D1796755

Dedication

For Steph, without whose help this tale would not be possible, my eternal gratitude. Don't panic, it's not in lieu of that tricycle you desire.

For Mom, you showed me how to survive with dignity, no matter what hand I am dealt.

For my friends murdered over the years in Fyzabad, our mischievous childhood memories live on.

CARNIVAL MIND DARK SOUL

Don Fabien

To Mavis & Tony,
Hope you enjoy!
Best wishes,
Don Fab
(Don Fabien)

AUSTIN MACAULEY
PUBLISHERS LTD.

Copyright © **Don Fabien** (2017)

The right of Don Fabien to be identified as author of this work has been asserted by him in accordance with section 77 and 78 of the Copyright, Designs and Patents Act 1988.

Edited by Stephany Choremi-Fabien

This is a work of fiction. While the literary perceptions are based on experiences, all names, characters, places, products, and incidents are either products of the author's imagination or are used fictitiously.

All rights reserved. No part of this publication may be reproduced, stored in a retrieval system, or transmitted in any form or by any means, electronic, mechanical, photocopying, recording, or otherwise, without the prior permission of the publishers.

Any person who commits any unauthorized act in relation to this publication may be liable to criminal prosecution and civil claims for damages.

A CIP catalogue record for this title is available from the British Library.

ISBN 9781787103429 (Paperback)
ISBN 9781787103436 (E-Book)
www.austinmacauley.com

First Published (2017)
Austin Macauley Publishers Ltd.
25 Canada Square
Canary Wharf
London
E14 5LQ

Table of Contents

Belief

Although we come from different backgrounds and ethnicities, undeniably, we are all still stardust.

Yes our beliefs vary, but our minds have the capacity to evolve. Today, more and more of us implore equality for all, conceding only to pluralistic peace – a freedom of sorts in its purest of forms.

Let our respect for each other continue to grow with our relentlessness to comprehend all we do not know.

Let our awe for liberation continue to heighten equally as we strive to rectify issues we continue to cause as a civilisation.

Is Story's Time

No radio, television or internet to distract, instead, *jus' ah good-ol' tale*.

All nonconformities are intentional, and like any artist, it would be gratifying to be judged only for my efforts.

My only ask is for the reader to imagine the temperature is a humid seventy-eight degrees Fahrenheit, you are sat around a roaring fire on a beach in the Caribbean under a contradictory sky; dark, but lit by the twinkling stars and the waxing crescent of the approaching moon. Encircled by friends, the one with the most vivid imagination and the scariest of voices is telling a tale.

As Mom would say, *'Is story's time.'*

Prologue

The last day I can clearly recollect is May the twenty-eighth 2016.

Since being here – in purgatory, for lack of a better word – the days and nights all seem to merge, time has ceased to exist. Enduring without food or water I wither away, still strangely unable to die. I am on my own. I have always been here on my own, as I always have been, still uncertain of where here is, or how I arrived.

Morbid voices and coarse, wolf-like groans could always be heard in the distance, at times too close for comfort. Initially, these uncertainties in this gloomy nothingness would induce shivers down my emaciated spine. Now I am accustomed to these spectral melodies that do not respond to my presence.

While searching for a way out, oblivion took shape in the form of a metaphysical mandapam. Within this structure a rostrum arose. I took to the platform and on an inexplicably odious stool, made from a decaying dwarf bending over touching his toes, I roosted. I feel no pain, nor any sensation as I lean into a charred and smouldering, unlevelled lectern. The stench from the rotting carcass and the eeriness of my surroundings feel unmistakably as though I am sat adrift, in the very recesses of my tormented mind. I discovered writing materials. Through the dirtiest of atmospheres I squint, hunched close to the scorched pages to scribble these accounts with my now cosmic continuation. I confess, this may have caused me to maunder slightly, but I profess, the accounts are as accurate as humanly possible.

Now I know who she is. Although infinitely lost and in this state of dismay, the haunting of her ubiquitous presence throughout my entire life raises the hair on the back of my neck. But who, or what, were the other creatures?

Perseverance
Is still now, ah still lost, buh meh mind take me back in time

Every life seems to be a puzzle and mine is no different, yet I harbour an overwhelming feeling it is conflictingly unlike most. More mysterious. Living life with the knowledge that a darkness follows me everywhere does not make it easy, but the delicate light that shadows in the form of a white hummingbird, helps make my conundrum of an existence confidently bearable. It was not always so.

For as long as I can remember I've had awful headaches that go on for weeks. They're blinding and bring with them a curtain of nausea and unexplainable visions. I see things that no one else around me sees; evil things that appear only to me. Sometimes the visions manifest as spiders still equipped with a thorax and abdomen, but with eight miniature human legs, a small human head with half a dozen black eyes and nostrils running like a snotty-nosed child in the dead of winter, but instead of mucus there are drippings of blood leaving behind a trail like *Hansel and Gretel*. At times it feels like my headaches are induced by the clanging of their visible fangs. On other occasions, it takes the form of a child covered in gauzes and blood, almost mummified, its flesh occupied by maggots on display where the gauzes are unravelling, eyes black as night, no teeth and coarsely grunting like a pig. Although this vision is the size of a three-year-old toddler and never speaks, it's the one I'm most afraid of.

The various creatures follow me from time to time, appearing without warning but bizarrely, never trying to hurt me nor communicate, just follow and observe. Whenever those devilish creatures appear a white hummingbird does the same. However, it's more friendly and always remains closer, the delicate stream of air from the movement of its wings caressing me as it circles. I feel safer when it appears and unlike the others, it speaks to me at times.

Silver, that is what I call her.

As a child I witnessed a demonic possession of a family member. Everyone seemed uncertain at the time whether it was actually demonic or a mental manifestation. Eventually, the powers that be, guided by superstition, decided the best course of action was an exorcism and luckily for this family member it was successful. I cannot recall the full events, but on that day I did understand that for many individuals – even those claiming to be creatures of faith – the truth was and may always be that seeing is believing. The events I witnessed and the knowledge of no one else being able to see the fictitious creatures that followed me, my inability to produce proof and my growing internal bias against the people around me, created a fear of being locked away in a padded cell; thus I never disclosed to anyone what I saw and still see. It created a lonely existence filled with obscurity, my sleepless nights and sleepwalking only adding to my turtle-like mood.

I awoke last night stood in my flatmate's bedroom.

'Are you seeing a *You hun ye gui*?' Calvin asked.

I can still remember opening my eyes and shaking my head feeling somewhat confused. 'What!'

'I think you were seeing a You hun ye gui.'

'What is that?'

'It literally means *wild ghosts*. Your eyes were closed and you were fighting off something, it was very convincing.'

I stood confused, looking around his room.

'Have I been sleepwalking again?'

He was sat on the edge of his bed and thinking back now, must have been more confused than I was, but he remained calm as usual.

'Yeah, I think you were, but it was different this time. I really think something was attacking you. I saw something, I'm sure,' he said again under his breath, perplexed.

My flatmate is a student just like myself. We study business administration together, are very like-minded and get along really well, making us great flatmates and friends. His name is Zhou Mingyang, Zhou being his family name. In China, the country of his birth, it's customary to place the patronymic first, but the truth is, his name is too difficult for those of us unaccustomed to the Chinese languages to pronounce, so, to our shame, he allows us to call him Calvin.

Leh we go further dong memory-lane

I was born in the San Fernando General Hospital on Saturday the twenty-eighth of May, 1983 and grew up in a small town in the Saint Patrick county of Trinidad called Fyzabad, not known to many but famed for the discovery of petroleum from below its grounds and for being the hometown of the talented musician, Billy Ocean. There's one other thing about Fyzabad considered to be of great importance: the statue of Tubal Uriah "Buzz" Butler on Charlie King Junction, as the locals call the site. This is where Fyzabad Road meets Guapo Road and I spent my early years, almost every day as I passed by, seeing the dark smiling figure in his bowler hat and three-piece suit, clutching in his left hand what appeared to be a bible. It was not until I was at university that I gained a more in-depth knowledge about the man—well, at least what was written about him.

What I did know previously was of his achievements within the trade unions as my grandparents and other locals would talk about him regularly. They would say he was a Spiritual-Baptist preacher and labour leader who mobilised and led the working class to prevail from harrowing social circumstances and practically slave-like conditions within the workplace – modern indentureship, without free passage or any form of long-term gain. Many people were working for an average of seven cents per hour. I know it was during the 1930's and the cost of living was cheaper, but to put it into perspective, within the US at the same time the average wage in northern cities was around fifty-three cents per hour, while southern cities paid an average of thirty-two cents per hour. My grandparents vocalised their beliefs of colonialism as the main cause of these injustices and they, as well as everyone else, desired home rule during those oppressive times. They believed the hunger strikes and fierce protests led by Buzz Butler helped to create hope and a strong viewpoint of an independent country as the main catalyst to improve the suffering that countless faced. He was not originally from Fyzabad, not even Trinidad; his country of birth was Grenada. Still, he used his influence to voice the need for change.

Both skilled and unskilled workers were abused and regarded as less than farm animals. They were not allowed the appropriate machinery to complete difficult tasks and suffered horrific injuries, especially the oil field workers. The most painful aspect for many was the conspicuous racist attacks made by the colonial rulers, one quoted as saying, "These black dogs only bark, they cannot bite." This was an openly apparent response to the threat of protest. Fyzabad was at the heart of their plight; the protests began there in the Apex Oilfields on June the nineteenth, 1937.

A police officer, Corporal Charlie King, travelled to Fyzabad with a warrant to arrest the accused main protagonist, Buzz Butler, but instead, Charlie King trudged head-on towards his own gruesome murder. Corporal King told me he had faced an angry mob tired of injustice.

'*Dey beat meh, bludgeoned meh, doused meh in kerosene and burn meh alive,*' he would often say to me. '*Dis kinda savagery towards ah innocent man trying tuh do 'e job, is wah give de junction its nickname today,*' he would always go on to add.

The protests continued and workers on bicycles spread the word like wildfire. It whipped through the island, involving labourers from the sugar and cocoa estates, oil fields, docks, railway, even store workers. It didn't come to a halt until July the second, 1937, only ending because British troops arrived on two battleships, the *Exeter* and the *Ajax*. Over a dozen people died. Order was imposed by the colonisers to end the *dis*order. It would not be until 1962 that Trinidad and Tobago would become an independent nation.

It's probably biased coming from me, but still, there's no place on earth like the Trinidad and Tobago, I know. Despite its bitter past, the people there are still amongst some of the friendliest I have ever encountered. Why shouldn't they be? A country always comfortably warm, the cardinal points protected in the north by three mountains, the south and west coasts protected by the South American landmass while the east coast, although facing the Atlantic Ocean, is still comfortably within the Caribbean Sea. Whenever a hurricane swirls into being, these natural protections are so effective that many

17

Trinidadians quip that *"God is ah Trinidadian."* The majority of Trinidad's beaches consist of dark-ish mineral-rich sands and emerald green waters, a fusion of the Orinoco Delta pouring into both the Caribbean and the Atlantic Sea causing a moss-like moat around the island. Tobago, while a separate isle, is more rural with creamy coral beaches, waters clear and calm, like a large warm puddle on a white terrazzo floor.

On many occasions, I've been told by foreigners that my place of birth is the wealthiest nation within the region, that there shouldn't be the extent of poverty that currently exists there. It's a fact which always makes me sad. Many of these numerous individuals don't have a clue what real poverty actually is. That's not necessarily a bad thing but without understanding the true amount of deprivation many face, in terms of not having the opportunities to acquire necessities, they still feel compelled to share and sometimes enforce their entitled opinions. Luckily the resilience of an innumerable amount of my mongrel-like people continue fighting to survive. Some go further, standing fearlessly for what is right: the first name which comes to mind – and certainly unknown to him but my mentor nonetheless – is Afra Raymond.

As a boy, I did not experience the level of deprivation my grandparents endured but that didn't mean it was a walk in the park for us either. My dad lived at a different address and from time to time he would turn up with gifts, trinkets, and sometimes books. I loved him for it. My mom I despised because I saw her as the authoritative figure and I felt as though she cared for my brother and sister more than she cared for me. We were somewhat happy, although never having much other than freedom.

Over the years Fyzabad changed again. The oil began diminishing and poverty crept back in like a thief in the night, just as it once had during the turmoils faced by my grandparents. Together with inflation the peaceful mirage dissipated and made visible the unavoidable truth: while growing up I began realising that unless you were from a highly connected or wealthy family, it was extremely hard to provide food and other basic necessities, such as water and electricity, for your family.

Signs of any form of economic aid or financial management of the country's assets were nowhere to be seen, even though the country had an estimated gross domestic product of nine billion dollars (USD) with an estimated population of 1.3 million people. Many were still living on less than a dollar (USD) a day. My opinion at the time was, and still is, anyone with authority would take what they wanted, leaving nothing for the people lower down the food chain. This continually happened across the different political parties who reigned over the years; honestly, it's impossible to say which one of them was the worst. *Clearly*, home rule turned out to be the equivalent of colonialism.

Trinidad and Tobago's elected democratic governments which were bestowed with power, by the people, to protect the people, was just an illusion. The majority of politicians created a cesspool of corruption which grew like Rome before its collapse. The poor suffered and still continue to suffer. A once unspoilt beautiful paradise, now at war within, expectedly awoke the sleeping giant of anger, bitterness and racism encouraged by the same politics, abusing the difference of ethnicity for its own personal gain. Due to these visible politically-made divides, disappointingly, most Afro-Trinidadians now support an Afro-majority party, whereas most Indo-Trinidadians support an Indian-majority party. This gave way to a race blame culture, as opposed to any individual being accountable for their own actions.

The people of this now-vanishing paradise, blinded by the colour of each other's skin, have allowed it to manifest into a land of hurt, hatred and jealousy. The various governments encouraged it and I was unfortunate enough to witness this first hand.

I could only imagine the difficulties my mom had actually been facing back then, a single parent with few opportunities, trying to care for all three of us and herself. It was not until becoming an adolescent with a better understanding of what was really going on around me, that I began to see the truth. My mom, in fact, did an amazing job of raising us while juggling work to put food on the table for my younger siblings and me. My dad lived just fifteen minutes away with another family, providing for them without a care in the world as to whether we were okay or not. Eventually, he emigrated to New York in the US and we lost contact with him for many years.

At the nearest point, South America is only seven miles away from Trinidad and Tobago and with such easy accessibility to the South American narcotics trade, drug-related crimes began manifesting as the only way out for many deprived young people, and it did not fall from my gaze. My immaturity didn't help either. As a means of coping with my broken life at that time, I vented my anger and frustration at everything and anything to the point where my mom, stretched to breaking point, could not control me or my behaviour anymore.

At seventeen I was sent to New York to stay with my father, despite barely knowing him and not seeing him for about six years. Disappointingly, he knew nothing of how to be a good father, nor did he even try, and I consequently had no idea how to be his son. Within four months I had to leave his home. I have a vivid memory of him handing me an envelope containing a return airline ticket to Trinidad and some cash. I refused to return to Fyzabad, although my mom and siblings were there; there was really nothing to return to, with few and dwindling opportunities for low-income families like us. I feared to return would make me a worse person, with nothing left for me other than a life of crime, prison or death, all fuelled by an internal desire for a better life. I reluctantly took the cash, left the airline ticket and ran without ever looking back.

I was pretty much alone in a strange new world but because it was of my own doing I was, for the most part, fearless, with the occasional hint of melancholy. Memories of my earlier years during the transformation that Trinidad and Tobago were undertaking was varied, but I could still remember days when time seemed to stand calmly, playing Bail with my cousins and neighbours who were as close as family.

Bail is a fantastic game; any number of people can play. We would fill a sixteen-ounce plastic Busta bottle with stones and place it in the centre of a small circle drawn on the ground. One person would have to be the catcher, close their eyes – no peeking – and count to an agreed number while everyone else scampered and hid.

The catcher would have to remain within line of sight to the circle housing the Busta bottle while discovering everyone's hiding place, one, two, even three at a time. When a hiding place was discovered the catcher would shout, "*Bail*!" while shaking the bottle and naming the discovered person or persons and their hideout. Loud maracas-like sounds would resonate from the bottle as it was being shaken, then the shouts of, "*Bail! Dondee, ah see yuh hiding by de Julie mango tree, come out nah!*" This would continue until everyone's hideout was discovered and the first person found would then become the catcher, but if anyone in hiding ran out, kicked or shook the bottle while the catcher was away from it hunting, the game would then start over and the catcher would have to catch again. We loved playing that game.

The end of my teenage years and early adulthood was spent not playing games, but instead surviving the Big Apple; not as glamorous as portrayed in the movies but in truth, I enjoyed most of it. Seven years passed during which, with a bit of elbow grease and luck, I had miraculously landed on my feet. Everything seemed to be great, I had an enjoyable well-paid job at a respectable firm and many new opportunities, both socially and professionally.

January 2015

The firm I worked for managed to weather the global financial crisis between 2007 to 2008 but seven years later it began to unravel and the company was forced to stop trading. It was not a good time for most of my work colleagues. Thankfully I had lived by a piece of advice my old math teacher had given us during high school back in Trinidad: *"Save as much as all yuh can, whenever yuh can, and always expect de rain."*

During that crossroads in my life, I met an elderly woman on the subway with whom I encountered the strangest experience – rich coming from me, I guess. I was on my way home on a cold January evening after a fun Saturday of retail therapy on Knickerbocker Avenue, an area I wasn't terribly familiar with but had heard it was a great place to buy trendy gear at discount prices. I had, however, also heard equally negative stories about how unsafe it could be at times, so I wanted to leave before it got dark. I boarded the L train, long before dusk, at Myrtle and Wyckoff Avenues heading towards 14th Street station. There was a free seat next to an elderly woman, so I sat.

'I like seeing young people smiling,' she said.

'Thank you,' I replied, still smiling.

'You have an engagement with destiny.'

'Really?' I replied matter-of-factly, while still trying to remain respectful. I was somewhat distracted looking up at the train's route display for my stop. I was seven stops away from Lorimer Street, where I would need to transfer to the G train, travel three stops towards Court Square, leaving me a few blocks away from my apartment in Long Island City.

'You're about to move to the United Kingdom,' she gently continued.

'That sounds exciting, but how do you know that?' I replied, frowning.

'I'm psychic. Give me your hand.'

Reluctantly, after a long shared pause, I placed my bags on the grubby train floor, clutched between my legs, jerky and quivering, uncertain if it was caused by the moving train or my nervousness. I surrendered my right hand.

'No, give me the other.'

I quietly obliged her. While clasping my hand gently between both of hers, she closed her eyes, becoming quiet and calm. After a few long seconds, her breathing began to change, it became increasingly laboured as though she were suffocating. I was now very aware of the curious stares from other passengers as the tension and the level of suspense began to rise throughout the train carriage. Before anyone had the chance to react she abruptly snatched her hands away, staring at me with an intensity I had never before encountered, then flew up out of her seat and hastily fled the carriage without looking back.

Everyone was left looking bewildered, staring in her direction, having witnessed what appeared to be some sort of escape. We watched her continue to move through the train then disappearing, it seemed, into a crowded carriage. I slowly sat back down. Most of the passengers were now staring at me. I heard a young boy ask his mom, 'What did that man do to that woman?'

She responded with a look that immediately indicated he be quiet. I ignored everyone, made my transfer and continued my journey home. This bit of the journey I knew well. Normally short, it went by even quicker than usual. When I reached the lobby of my building I absentmindedly headed down the short staircase into the mail room. I liked this room, it imitated a bank vault with a huge round metal door to complete the effect, but designed to remain permanently open. The room was completely clad in black marble except for a wall of sandblasted steel-finished post boxes that I unconsciously acknowledged were always cold, despite the warm rays from the sunken spotlights in the ceiling. I typed my password into the digital display and my box opened; there was just one letter. I had applied to different universities to study international business and as I stared down at the British postmark and the Queen Elizabeth stamps, I realised it must be the response from Plymouth University in the United Kingdom. While my mind ran on the predictions of the psychic on the train, I left the mail room and wandered towards the lift as I opened the envelope, the contents of which confirmed my place at

Plymouth University to study a BA (Hons) in Business Administration for the next three years, starting that September, 2015. Excited by the letter I attempted to convince myself that the events of my subway ride, although strange, were just a coincidence. I brushed it off in the manner one would when reading one's horoscope segment in a newspaper. Then it hit me; this could be a sign, being that my life is not as conventional as most. I had hoped Silver would show up so that I could safely confide in her and listen to what she thought but it didn't really matter, I had already made up my mind. I would accept the place with Plymouth University and I was going to the UK to study, no matter how much that lady had freaked me out. Still, the worry of spending all my savings on going to university was there, constantly on my mind, but I had a plan and it would work out. I had to be confident; a degree would give me the opportunity to obtain a better job.

Normally most Trinidadians, Caribbean people or even Mexicans in my position would religiously send what little money they earned back to their home country via Western Union or Money Gram for their relatives. Many lived in meagre accommodation, sometimes without heating or proper meals to achieve their goal of sending a better life to their families, but it was rarely enough to truly help or really make a difference. I admired this greatly but could not agree with it. I felt they needed to strengthen themselves and focus on sustaining their ability to provide. A lot of the hard-working people I witnessed sending all their earnings to their home countries would eventually burn out, having struggled to survive the harshness that life continually allowed to occur. The work we found was never easy; many workers were abused, belittled or taken advantage of and as illegal immigrants, we had very few choices and no rights nor power to complain, contrary to what many governments would like you to believe.

Some people took advantage of the US educational opportunities available to better themselves long term. The education system allows for anyone to do a GED, a diploma in General Educational Development and when acquired, certifies that the individual has met the high school level of academic skills required to get by. This piece of paper didn't help everyone but it did help many, especially those who had arrived without a proper education. It gave me an opportunity to acquire a better job, with a manager who was caring and generous. There were some people who considered this qualification to be a waste of time but when these individuals had had enough and threw in the towel, deciding to return to their home country because life in the western world had not turned out to be quite what they had expected, it would be at a loss and still poorly educated.

I had known people who had sent every penny they earned to their loved ones, enough to support them and entrusting the rest of their money to them to save, but when they eventually returned home all the money was gone. I knew someone who had arrived home unannounced to surprise his family only to find his wife living in their family home with another man; she even had a new baby for this fellow. This new live-in boyfriend did not even have a job but instead was comfortably kept by the US dollars being sent home by the wife's hard-working husband. I knew my mom to be a responsible woman and I still sent money for her whenever I could, just not as regularly as everyone else who sent money home to their families. I wanted to strengthen and educate myself first. Once in a financially stable and safer position, with a better job, I would finally be able to look after her and my siblings properly.

Every illegal immigrant I encountered living and working in New York City had goals. Many wanted to return to their place of birth with a bag full of money to retire with. It hardly ever worked out like that for most. The cost of city life would take its toll; in fact, I think many never accounted for the trials that life brings with it; illness, even death, leaving their families to beg and borrow to cover transportation costs in order to move their cold bodies back to their homeland. Sadly some remained as a "Doe". The majority would end up doing jobs they hated just to keep paying the bills and to be able to send a yearly barrel filled with snacks, clothes, the odd bit of bed linen and whatever useful items could be found in a sale. This posted cylinder was always a joy to receive no matter what was in it, but I wanted to give my family more than this.

The strangest thing was, I could not even remember what the psychic woman on the train looked like. By the time I got out of the lift any recollection of her features was completely gone. I entered my apartment puzzled; how could I completely forget a character like that? I wouldn't be able to pick her out if she were stood in a police line-up directly in front of me, no matter how much I tried. Oh well, I thought and placed the day's events in the recesses of my mind as I began to get undressed to try on my new clothes. I was about to be on my own once more in a new country, entirely of my own choice.

'F@#k it!' I shouted out loud, as I pulled up a new pair of jeans.

Colonialism

The policy or practice of acquiring full or partial political control over another country, occupying it with settlers, and exploiting it economically.

Virgin
Still dong memory-lane, May 2015

It was now May the twenty-eighth, my thirty-second birthday. I had subleased my apartment to a lovely couple, taken my savings and got on a Virgin Atlantic flight, leaving New York City behind. Somewhat spoilt by the attention from the attentive flight attendants – *Yeah, ah think ah did leh it slip out dat it was meh birthday jus' tuh get attention from de gorgeous stewardesses* – I thoroughly enjoyed the flight. The food was surprisingly good for an airline and the inflight entertainment, both social and digital, kept me occupied and passed the time away perfectly.

I landed and I didn't even get searched. This country is great! I thought after only being here fifteen minutes. I passed through border control, completely dignified but confused as to why the officers were so polite. In every other country I have travelled to, I've been searched and treated like a potential terrorist, maybe because I'm brown-skinned and I smile at border control. I can't help smiling, I'm a nice person, I think, and I don't agree with terrorism just as much as any other non-terrorising person.

After cheerfully finding my bearings I boarded my pre-booked train at Heathrow Terminal Five to Plymouth. The journey was just over four hours long but very comfortable; the views of green England and its seaside towns along the way added to my excitement of this new adventure. I arrived at my new apartment just as the sun was setting over Plymouth; it was strangely gloomy but beautifully different to what I had been accustomed to.

Plymouth is a small city on the south coast of Devon, England, about one hundred and ninety miles south west of London. Some early history extends to the Bronze Age when a first settlement emerged and continued as a trading post for the Roman Empire until it transcended to become the more prosperous village of Sutton, now known as Plymouth. In 1620, the Pilgrim Fathers departed Plymouth for the New World and established Plymouth Colony, the English settlement which helped to forge the nation we know today as the United States of America.

Although the city may be steeped in history it can appear to be a bit of a bore, this is actually not the case and the list of restaurants and bars is quite sufficient for an enjoyable night out. I even heard the university is able to boast the second largest Student Union bar and facilities in the country. Many may seem to think that Plymouth University is in its infancy but believe me, it is only the name change over the years that could have conjured up that image. The university's roots can easily be traced back to almost two hundred years ago and has rapidly evolved, producing some of the best degree courses and lecturers in the world, with the accolades and research to back up that claim. I learnt all this information after arriving. Before, I had only known mostly the economic and statistical side of my destination, new up-to-date stats and figures were not available but the previous year the university was ranked forty-ninth in the UK by the *Guardian* and sixty-fifth by the *Complete University Guide*. The cost of living in Plymouth was not great, but more affordable than most of the other UK cities I had researched. Overall, it was the safest bet.

At thirty-two, some may call me a late bloomer but it would have been foolish of me not to capitalise on my new-found academic opportunities. I had been a high school dropout and cannot even sum up the words to describe how I disliked school in my younger years. I was now a Trinidadian expatriate living in Plymouth, with few connections to what was rapidly becoming a distant memory of my old home in Trinidad and Tobago.

I decided to move to Plymouth in May to settle in during the summer before my first semester began in September. I arranged a flat share through an estate agent with another student; he was much younger but happened to be enrolled on the same course as myself. Calvin was his name. We chatted on the phone and got along like a house on fire before even meeting. He had planned to do the same as I, by moving to Plymouth during early summer.

The beginning of our summer was great, spending much of our time exploring the south west. I visited a town called Exmouth which I loved, situated on the east coast of Devon, offering a diverse selection of things to do including great water sports, fantastic routes for cycling and walking, internationally acclaimed nature reserves as well as two miles of stunning beach that is great whatever the weather. I didn't know quite what to expect regarding British weather, except for what I absorbed as a child watching *Mary Poppins*. It rained for most of my first summer here but I enjoyed it anyway.

While exploring the beautiful beach in Exmouth I met an elderly woman. Her facial features were very defined and unforgettable, strangely rugged for a woman; she was not Caucasian. If I had to hazard a guess, I would say she may be Native American. We introduced ourselves; she had a strong accent which I struggled to understand when she spoke quickly. Her name was Malliouhanna, she had to spell it for me and it did take a few attempts before I could pronounce it properly.

'What does your name mean?'

'An arrow-shaped sea serpent,' she replied.

Her smile emerged, maliciously playful, but her demeanour was as friendly as everyone else I had encountered in this south west region of England, but despite Malliouhanna being a complete stranger, there was something about her that seemed very familiar. Recognising from my accent that I was a Trinidadian national, she became excited and began talking about Trinidad and Tobago carnival celebrations.

Trinidad carnival has always been described as an explosion of colour, music, revelry, and creativity. It has spawned similar celebrations around the world, such as Notting Hill Carnival in London, but as every Trinidadian knows and anyone who has ever experienced Trinidad's remarkable fusion of sun, sweat, music, food and smiles merged within a plethora of colours, nothing on earth can rival the euphoria and stunning spectacle of this festival.

Malliouhanna experienced Trinidad carnival in her youth and could remember the massive masquerade bands, spectacular costumes, unparalleled fetes all fuelled by folklore, and the pulsating sounds of steel-pan, calypso and soca music. She explained that after returning to her homeland, life had changed, never giving her the opportunity to return to Trinidad and Tobago but she was still able to reminisce the ecstasy felt during her stay and the irresistible music she frolicked to day and night.

'Ah calypso, sweet calypso music,' she lilted. Her face lifted up towards the sun on the Devonshire beach, she looked at me. 'The sun just isn't the same, is it.'

'No, it isn't,' I replied, screwing up my face playfully and pondering the thought.

Calypso is a fusion of sounds adapted from an introduction of West African kaiso, introduced to the island by French planters and their slaves. With time and as English replaced Patois or Creole French as the dominant language, calypso migrated into English and with more time, it evolved and created another genre called soul calypso or soca, which now has a hold on most of the English-speaking Caribbean.

Being young and up-to-date with this genre, I love soca music. *Meh two favourite musicians Alison Hinds and Super Jigga TC, buh meh two bess ones is Machel Montano and Bunji Garlin. Both have different sounds; Machel, energetic and colourful, embodying one-half ah carnival and Bunji, raw and dark, encapsulating de other side ah carnival culture.*

Maybe it was my subconscious thought of the Caribbean heat but the British summer sun was too much for my brown skin to bear, I had to flee to the shade before combusting. My new friend chuckled as we said our goodbyes. I began walking off the beach while I continued to reminisce to myself about Trinidad and Tobago. It had now been fifteen years since I'd left, all of my adult life, but I still felt one hundred percent Trinidadian. The thought made me smile.

As I continued to ponder my life from Trinidad to the US to England a feeling rushed towards me like a landslide, it was her! The psychic from the subway in New York, five months previously. I swung around, looking back, genuinely scared. She was gone. Where did she go? There was nothing behind me other than the sea.

The rest of the summer went gradually downhill. I started my course; the assignments and exams became a welcome distraction. Christmas came and went. Spring popped up every now and again amongst the dark, cold, wet days like an annoying foretaste of the upcoming summer. My visions continued, becoming more severe. Silver's visits were less frequent and I began feeling unsafe. Normally I was able to ignore the creatures I saw but something was different, their presence seemed to be growing more powerful. It affected me to the point that I feared leaving my apartment. I had begun visiting mystics, psychics, tarot readers; anyone that I thought could possibly help. This was not cheap, I was spending all my disposable income on any form of hope. I needed a part-time job to earn a bit of extra income in what, I was also quickly discovering, is probably one of the most expensive countries to live in.

I eventually found a job a few minutes away from the university and the flat that I shared with Calvin. I started working as a part-time care assistant in a home for mentally disabled patients. It was completely different to anything I had ever experienced before and had me extremely confused and unaware of what to expect at the start of each shift. At times the work would feel self-rewarding; other shifts could leave you emotionally drained after dealing with severe illness or impending death, then bizarrely another touching, sentimentally humorous moment would make you laugh until you cried. I was uncertain whether this was the safest environment for me but I needed the money to continue funding my search for a glimpse of light at the end of my darkening tunnel. Each resident was different and had all lived amazing lives with the most incredible stories to tell. One elderly woman was the main attraction at a circus for many years as she would drive her motorcycle through an extremely small ring of fire. Another had been a spy, and so on.

Twenty-first ah May 2016

I only worked during weekends and overall really enjoyed it, especially after one particular resident arrived, Kairi Lele, who insisted we call him Kai.

Kai was an eighty-two-year-old gentleman of mixed race, just like myself, and unbelievably youthful in both manner and looks. I'm not sure I would even have said he was fifty years old; he was almost unnatural and would make playful remarks about his looks.

'Black don't crack,' he would quip. Everyone thought it was funny but we were all too scared to repeat it, now that everyone had to be so politically correct.

He suffered from a mental disability and was unable to care for himself due to unexpected hallucinations. After reading his fascinating file I was excited and eager to chat to him as our similarities were uncanny. The weekends were always short-staffed and tended to be extremely manic at times, dealing with all the different needs of the residents, allowing very little time to have a lengthy chat with any one person. Eventually, there was a quiet spell for fifteen minutes before the end of one of my shifts, when Kai and I were able to talk. I ran up to his room and knocked on his door. A warm voice invited me in and as I entered he smiled.

'I was expecting you,' he said.

He was sat in an armchair, about to place the book he was reading on a side cabinet. I quickly apologised for disturbing his reading but with the same welcoming smile he calmly replied, 'You're not disturbing me, I knew you were coming up for a chat.'

I did find his comment a little strange but I made myself comfortable, seated on the floor in front of him, and began chitchatting. I told him we had the same birthday and were both from the same Caribbean island. The conversation escalated and the similarities began mounting, from our love of Caribbean cuisine and drinks to the extent of how much we missed that warm climate and most of all, carnival. While conversing, the recognition of curiosity grew between us. We both wanted to know what brought each of us to cold, rainy Devon. Kai sat up in his armchair, with a worrying frown and without hesitation he asked, 'Why are you here?'

He listened intently to my story and as I finished he responded, '*Your* story has only just begun.'

I hope so, I innocently thought, there are so many things I long to see and do before my life ends; then, like an eager young child, I continued, 'What about you? What brought you here?'

Still smiling, he replied, 'I don't think we would have enough time today for my story.'

I glanced at my watch and realised it was already 8.10p.m.

'My shift ended ten minutes ago but if you're not too tired, I would love to stay a while to hear your story.'

He sat back in his chair. 'So you want me to tell you the story of my life?'

Consumed with curiosity and intrigue, my head nodded in acceptance.

Land Of The Hummingbird

I was born on the intriguing island of Trinidad in the Caribbean on the twenty-eighth of May, 1933, as you already know, and Stephen, my father worked for a private organisation within the oil industry. Asphalt had already been discovered by Sir Walter Raleigh in 1595, the island's source dubbed the Pitch Lake and immediately put to use as caulk for his ships. In 1857 within the vicinity of the pitch lake, the first well was drilled for oil sixty-one metres deep.

My mother died during my birth. In our home, I remember a black and white photograph of a woman I wish I had known. She did not have any surviving family and I knew almost nothing about her other than what my distant and ambiguous father would rarely share. She was of Garifuna descendant or Black Carib, these were a mixture of the island's first inhabitants before its rediscovery by Christopher Columbus in 1498 and the free Africans who populated the Caribbean, due to the Spanish King's Cedula of Population in 1776 and 1783. What my father did share was that my mother was an outstanding example of an exotic flower. She possessed a natural beauty without any synthetic pretences. To my understanding of beauty at that young age, I felt that the photograph of her we possessed proved it.

I was named by my mother; or at least, as my father told me, it was what she wanted my name to be, Kairi, its origins being Kalinago, the language of my mother's indigenous past relatives, the Caribs. It simply means "Land of the Hummingbird" but my friends call me Kai.

My father's surname and now my own is Lele, also Kalinago, which interestingly means the exact same thing as my first name. My father told me my mother was fascinated by the mystery of his name and his family history because it was unknown to him and he was Caucasian. She thought his name and their meeting was some sort of strange and interesting fate, but he knew nothing of his family, nor had any; he had been raised in an orphanage in New York without a clue of his origin. Despite his humble upbringing, he was still a gentleman by anyone's standards and the local women adored him, but I don't think he ever gave any one of them the time of day, I think he truly loved my mother.

After she passed away, my father made a promise to my mother and himself that he would try his best to raise me in the Caribbean, which would offer me a more relaxed and safer childhood, something he himself never had, but I also felt this was his way of keeping me close to her. It was true, my life was unmistakably comfortable, without a care in the world, but everything changes.

1945. I was twelve years old and it was the year that changed my life forever, the beginning of the end. I am still not sure if it was for the better or worse but I believe it did carve me into who I am today.

At that time we lived in a small village in south Trinidad, called Fyzabad. It was a magical place, vegetation everywhere, lush with amazing shades of green dotted with the most vibrant colours of fragrant flowers and fruits.

As Kai described his hometown my face lit up. 'We're even from the same town!' I exclaimed, quickly apologising and asking him to continue.

He smiled and went on.

There was one main road running through the village, like a river carving its way through the landscape, a couple of streets branching off and numerous paths created through the vegetation and bull grass from constant use by the villagers. I loved these paths, the sound of the wind blowing through the trees and the mesmerising sway of the grass. My father and I lived in a cottage, or townhouse; I was never quite sure what the correct description of the house was. As a child it reminded me of the gingerbread house from the fairytale *Hansel and Gretel*, pretty and ornate, unfortunately not edible but instead made of timber.

I attended a primary school not more than fifteen minutes' walk away from our home and many of my classmates and friends lived in houses along the paths branching off the main road. My father would leave for work before I awoke every morning, leaving the nanny to look after me and always returned home around the same time, just before dusk. Her name was Maria, a local woman from the village who lived in with us. She was more of a mother figure than a nanny, from whom I received, and would like to think I returned, the feeling of overwhelming love. I had the utmost respect for her and was always looked after with the best of care. I had the freedom of a bird and could go or do almost anything as long as I went to school every day, did my homework before going off on adventures with my friends, and abided by a specific rule my father laid down, to return home before dusk, but we were still allowed to be out in the garden. My friends and I used this time to get more intimate with our coal pot, mostly to roast cashew seeds, the smell being splendidly disgusting.

At times we made what we called popguns, constructed from three pieces of bamboo. The first piece or barrel came from between the bamboo notches and was about a foot long. The wall of the bamboo was thick and the inner hole was always small. The second piece or pusher came from a thinner piece of bamboo and without any joints that would fit into the inner hole of the barrel. The third piece was an off-cut of the barrel only a couple of inches long, containing a joint and one end of the pusher was shoved in towards the joint to avoid a sharp pointy end. After constructing our popguns we would go looking for a particular fruit tree, a *Pommerac* or rose apple tree, the flowers being the perfect size for our gun barrels and always plentiful, the ideal ammunition.

The pusher was always an inch or so shorter than the barrel and the first flower would be inserted into the small hole. After pushing it down the barrel with the pusher and sending the flower lower into the chamber, the pusher would then be removed and a second flower could be lodged, repeating the process, but this time, *very* gently.

The pressure would shoot out the first flower like a bullet at painful speeds. We squealed with laughter and excitement when we shot each other playing games like Cops and Robbers.

Summers were the best, no school or homework. Armed with our popguns our wings would spread and we would take flight, exploring everywhere and everything all together, but never failing to always return home before the gathering darkness. Dusk was magical and my favourite time of the day: the colours of the noctilucent clouds hovering in the twilight; the glances and flutters of bats awakening; the almost certain appearances of fireflies in every direction both beautiful and mesmerising, leaving punctures of light in the emerging darkness.

Douens

One Thursday evening, it all changed. The sunset was premature. I was on my way home, racing through a bush path when I noticed children in the distance, playing. As I inquisitively approached they dispersed and hid in the greenery. It seemed rather strange and I could not understand why and where they ran off to. They appeared to be quite young and probably should not have been out on their own this late. I called out to the children numerous times but there was no reply, it was as if they just vanished and I was both confused and bewildered.

It suddenly dawned on me that it was getting darker and a curtain of fright blew over me. The night in Trinidad is not always as dark as you might think; the moon and stars provided abundant light and I noticed how they seemed closer in the sky than in other countries that I had visited with my father.

The bushes all around me rustled and what appeared to be two young children stood at arm's-length away from me but I observed the strangest thing. They seemed to be androgynous and their faces were hidden by some sort of mask—as a matter of fact, their faces appeared to be blurred. I was startled but at the same time curious. I could hear Maria calling out to me and like some kind of magic trick, whatever it was that stood in front of me immediately vanished once more. I stood dazed, weak at the knees. All I could think of was to run as quickly as my wobbly knees would carry me, straight towards Maria's voice, out of the bush path towards home.

Maria was stood with her arms folded waiting for me. She was not annoyed at my late arrival but looked worried. She quickly enquired as to what was the matter. I caught my breath.

'Nothing, I got carried away playing a game and was rushing to get home, which made me a bit distressed.'

Pausing for a moment, she looked at me disbelievingly. *'Yuh father is already in de house and annoyed with yuh. Yuh should get washed and ready fuh dinner.'*

When I arrived at the table my father had started dinner without me. I apologised and he nodded with acceptance as I sat. I ate slowly, thinking about my strange encounter earlier that evening and although I was scared I knew I had to return to the scene. What were they? I thought.

The night was warm and Maria must have come in, as she usually did, to open my window shutters with the hope of keeping me cool and comfortable as I slept.

A light breeze blew through my white linen curtains as I began stirring early the next morning to the chirps of kiskadees. My peaceful awakening was alarmed by an insect-like buzzing of something entering through the gap between the curtains. It was just a hummingbird, so beautiful but completely white. I had never seen one like this before. It whizzed around my room then vanished as quickly as it had entered. It made me straightaway remember what had happened the night before. Like lightning a thought bolted through my mind: there was a very old lady in the village, superstitious and entertaining. She would talk of strange and mysterious spirits living in the forest. Her exact age was uncertain to everyone: she had no teeth and could barely see; just enough to still get around. I got washed and dressed as quickly as I could and rushed over to her house. I knew she would already be awake lying in a hammock in her garden behind the house, away from prying eyes. Although she would relax in private, it was common knowledge she would be there very early, every morning, with an unusually large mortar and pestle beside her which everyone found very strange and generated a lot of curious gossip.

Her house was not very far away and similar to ours but unpainted, older and in dire need of repair. It looked extremely creepy, like a witch's house, but unlike my friends I was not scared of her. I liked her strange behaviour and enjoyed her quirky sense of humour. She fascinated me; I could only imagine the things she must have seen and done during her lifetime. The old lady was short, always clad in the same black skirt and white short-sleeved floral blouse dotted with patchwork repairs. Her flowing dreadlocks were always neat and tidy, riddled with a variety of beads. I once heard Maria disapprovingly say that the excessive wrinkles on the old woman's face were due to her over-indulgence of her ghastly cigarettes. Her nose was not aquiline like the familiar images of witches; instead, flatter and broader at the bridge, accompanied by sad, sunken eyes. Both her pain and wisdom were transferred with a single stare from those piercing orbs, the broken windows into her soul.

I arrived at her house and as predictable as the summer sun, Ms Hilda was sat in her hammock, upright as if on a bench, swinging in the slight early morning breeze. She gave me a welcoming smile then asked why I was not afraid of her.

'Everyone seems to think you're a soucouyant. This can't be true.'

She chuckled as she lit a cigarette and drew on it long and hard.

'*Ah soucouyant, chile,*' she explained through a puff of smoke, '*also known as ah ol' hag—*' she leant towards me, '*is ah supernatural being who has made ah pact with de devil tuh be able tuh change herself into many different forms.*'

She told me of their ability to cast spells on people to turn them into animals and of the many covenants one can make with evil if one only knows how. At night a soucouyant will shed her human skin and transform into a ball of fire, but must slip back into her skin before first light and the cock crows, otherwise, she will not be able to get back into it. She winked as she slowly eased back again. She continued to tell me that normally when people suspect an old woman in the village is, in fact, a soucouyant, they wait until the old hag leaves her house at night in a ball of flames, then pour salt onto the skin left behind in her mortar, making it shrink, leaving the creature unable to re-enter her skin, causing her to wither and die in the impending dawn.

Her story fascinated me and the way she told it made it even more convincing. I confided in Ms Hilda about my encounter with the strange mystery children and after hearing my description of what I had seen she hesitantly replied, '*Dey were douens.*' I begged her to explain and somewhat reluctantly she continued.

'*Douens are de roaming souls ah children who died before dey were baptised and doomed tuh roam de earth forever. Yuh'll find dem playing in forests and near rivers. De peculiar ting 'bout dem is dat dey have no faces and dey foot turned backwards. Dey may come near houses at night, crying and whimpering, mainly tuh approach children with de intention ah leading dem astray into de forest until dey are good and lost. Lonely,*' she murmured. '*Ah tink dey lonely and dey have de ability tuh forcefully make children stay with dem forever. Yuh must never leh douens hear yuh name. Dis will prevent dem from calling yuh at dusk, forcing yuh into ah trance-like state and attempting tuh lure yuh into de forest.*'

Horribly it dawned on me that the previous evening Maria had been calling me home and they must certainly have heard my name. Terror washed over my expression.

'*Doh worry,*' Ms Hilda reassured with a grandmotherly tone. '*Ah knew yuh mother very well and made ah unsaid vow tuh always protect yuh.*' Then, with a naughty chuckle, she sent me off to enjoy the day, only asking that I forget about what I had seen and not return to that place. I nodded in agreement, told her I was going to find my friends and ran off.

All day, as I tried to occupy myself I could think of nothing else but those faceless *picknies*. I imagined Maria calling me and when I would try to go in the direction of her voice I would be ambushed and taken away into the forest by the douens. I had to act, I could not let that happen and as the day was coming to an end and dusk approached, I decided to find them in the hope of reasoning with them. After all, they were children just like me, but lonely and probably sad.

Fear transformed itself into courage as I ventured towards the location where I had seen the creatures the day before. Disregarding what Ms Hilda had asked of me, I arrived just as dusk approached. No one, no creature was in sight. I waited patiently, sitting on a tree root, perturbed by the upcoming darkness. Just when my anxiety forced me to feel I could wait no more I stood, about to walk away, when they abruptly appeared. As they approached I staggered, speechless.

Before I could find the words to reason with them more appeared. Six, twelve? I quickly lost count as they rushed towards me, scratching me, hitting me, pushing me. I fell hard, hitting my head on a rock. I curled up in a fetal position as they approached my defenceless body, about to lay siege in the new darkness when abruptly, a meteorite ball of fire intervened. It violently bashed into the douens, scattering them until I was out of harm's way, then calmly continued to circle me while I lay on the ground drifting in and out of consciousness. Was this a dream?

The unnerving feeling of my eyes struggling to open in a bright light as I heard my name called out, was the first sign of morning. Eventually, I came round, but the sick feeling of fear and memories of my ordeal rushed back within me. What had saved me? I thought. Was it Ms Hilda?

I believed she really was a soucouyant and had kept her promise. I began frantically looking around for her. It was morning and I knew she could not survive if she had not made it back to her mortar to retrieve her skin before first light. I heard my name called out again, afraid to answer for fear it was more douens. I turned to run home. My dad was there, standing in front of me. He and a search party had been looking for me all night. His eyes were filled with tears. He walked up to me, hugged me, squeezed me close to him with both anxiety and relief, then lifted and cradled me towards his chest. Curled up in his arms like an infant, he carried me home.

Maria bathed me and smeared my bruises with what smelt like coconut oil; many Caribbean people use it as a liniment. It didn't really work, I was still sore and quietly went off to bed. Maria checked on me some time after but although it was now around midday, I was still so scared and could not sleep. After trying to comfort me she left my room. I closed my eyes and pulled my blanket up over my head. As I drifted in and out of a light sleep, flashbacks kept occurring of the faceless creatures attacking me and the menacing but controlled ball of fire encircling. I screamed out with fear. Both Maria and my father ran into my room. They calmed me, reassuring me I was not on my own and eventually I fell asleep for a while.

Soup

I awoke and jumped up with the comprehension that it would have been my fault if Ms Hilda had not made it back in time to retrieve her skin. My exhausted father was asleep on a chair in my room, and there was still daylight. I knew he would not let me out on my own, but I decided to ignore the voice of my conscience and sneak out of the house while he was dormant. I quietly climbed out of bed, picked up my slippers and tiptoed out of my room. Maria was nowhere to be seen so I made a clean break for it, straight to Ms Hilda's old wooden house.

When I arrived, breathless from my haste, it was very quiet apart from a low hum. I followed the ominous sound to the back of her house where we had been chatting the previous day. Covering my mouth and nose from the swarming flies, I warily approached her mortar and made the grimmest of discoveries. It was filled with a wretched-smelling, smouldering, bloody and maggot-infested soup. I ran inside her house, full of more flies. I searched all the rooms but could not find her. Now oblivious to the deafening flies circling, guilt-stricken, I collapsed to my knees, knowing that the mortar was filled with all that remained of her, and it was all my doing.

Although consumed with grief, I composed myself and ventured back home, not wanting to be caught outdoors after dark again, especially without Ms Hilda's protection. Even before my father's figure on the porch was in clear view, I could tell from his body language he was enraged and in truth, I was expecting no less. Approaching sheepishly with an apology, I sat next to him and told him everything from beginning to end, not missing a single detail. After I finished there was a long silence. Without saying a word, he stood up and walked into the house. I was not expecting that reaction. Somewhat bewildered, it took me some time before I realised he was not coming back and the conversation was over. In that moment I became aware of my fatigue from the distressing events of the day. I took a long, hot shower, scrubbing my body clean from the invasive flies which had covered me after feasting on the spine-chilling soup. As soon as my head hit the pillow I fell into a deep sleep, but haunted by dark forces.

I awoke, damp with sweat, to voices outside my bedroom door. I recognised one of the voices as my father's but the second male voice I could not identify. I went to see who was at our house so early on a Sunday morning. It was Doctor Rampersad, the family doctor and a long term friend of ours. He greeted me and asked if we could have a chat about the events that had occurred over the past two days. We both went back into my room and my father left to allow us some privacy. Dr Rampersad sat on a chair. I perched on the edge of my bed, both palms nervously rubbing my knobbly knees. He asked me to tell him what had happened and reassured me I could tell him the truth without having to worry about any repercussions and that he would try to help me. Reluctantly, I began telling the exact story I had told to my father. Sat at my writing desk, he seemed relaxed, listening intently and did not interrupt me, not once.

As I finished my story he stood calmly, thanked me for my honesty, then politely and jovially excused himself and went to speak to my father. They remained on the porch, talking for some time before Dr Rampersad eventually took his leave.

My father told me he had to run some errands and under no circumstances was I to leave the garden. He also informed Maria that she was not to let me out of her sight. I had expected this imprisonment after abusing their trust so I spent the day occupying myself at home, mostly playing in the swimming pool. Several times I noticed Maria deliberately ignoring me, pretending to be too busy to catch my eye. This sparked my curiosity but I shrugged it off, trying not to feel hurt. I just presumed she was annoyed with me.

Later that afternoon, all prune-like, I was sitting on the porch reading when my father returned. Maria came out when she heard his car; we both watched in silence as he drove through the ornately carved wooden gateway. Having got out of the car, he sauntered towards us, looking slightly apprehensive. Without acknowledging me he asked her if I was packed and ready.

'*Yes, ah jus' finished packing de bags while 'e was reading.*'

Startled, I asked where was I going, my voice shrill with distress.

'To your aunt in New York,' my father replied abruptly. He offered no other explanation than that I needed to see a doctor because I was not very well and would receive better treatment in New York. He began to walk away, leaving me engulfed in rage.

I was furious and not for being dumped with someone else, but because I never knew I had any other family. I demanded to know, where did my father miraculously, *abracadabra* from thin air, this mysterious aunt I knew nothing about? He turned around calmly to look at me before answering, and I saw a look of remorse cross his face as he recognised the underlying fear that was burning in my eyes. He gently knelt on the ground in front of me and for the first time was not abrupt nor tough, as he would normally be towards me. Instead, he seemed genuine, fatherly and when he spoke his voice seemed vulnerable; it shuddered and his eyes revealed a great sadness.

'She's not really your aunt, but she will treat you as if you are her nephew and you must respect her as if she were your family. Her name is Nancy and she's the only person other than Maria I would trust to look after you.'

Smiling reassuringly, he gently tapped my cheek, stood up and continued on into the house. A little comforted, but still in shock, I went inside to make sure Maria had packed the few things I treasured.

Shortly after organising myself for the journey I was taken to an airstrip, I think it was the airport. Normally, whenever I travelled with my father we would use a cruise ship but because the world had been at war for almost six years, commercial cruisers were not running as normal. The war never affected us in Trinidad and Tobago, or so it seemed to a protected child. I did not even realise the degree of the conflict until years after it had ended. I really was sheltered. My father explained he had arranged a private aircraft to take me to New York. It all happened so quickly.

As we arrived, men were transporting crates on board the aircraft from two vans.

'Fresh fruits, vegetables and provisions for the household,' my father said calmly. He held my hand as we walked up the staircase and took me on board. An assigned air stewardess was standing at the entrance, her sole purpose to look after me for the entire duration of the journey. Her name was Elizabeth. The fuselage was luxuriously comfortable, sixteen seats, I counted them. Two seats were free, the other fourteen were occupied with the crates containing the fresh produce. We went into the cockpit to meet the pilots.

'Welcome aboard,' one of them greeted me. 'You're flying in a Douglas DC-3 today. We have to make one fuel stop and the weather looks fantastic.' They introduced themselves but in my sombre mood I did not feel like responding, nor did I remember their names. They exchanged pleasantries with my father before he took me back to my seat.

'Elizabeth will take exceptional care of you,' he said as we approached her.

It was the strangest Sunday evening, I remember it as if it were yesterday. I remember the hug he gave me before he settled me into my seat and buckled my seatbelt. He whispered that he loved me and heartbreakingly, it was to be the last time I heard his voice without the aid of a telephone.

Idlewild

We landed at Idlewild airport during the night, now known as JFK, renamed in 1963 in memory of John F. Kennedy, the thirty-fifth President of the United States of America. Elizabeth had tried to chat to me, even tried to make me laugh, but at that time I was a very unhappy child. Leaving my father and Maria still feels like one of the hardest things I was ever forced to do. I was also consternated about what awaited me in New York and what medical treatment I apparently needed. I was given a full meal but could not really eat it, just snacked occasionally. My seat was very comfortable and I slept on and off throughout the flight, uncertain whether the turbulence was real or not.

At Idlewild, a stewardess took me to a lounge together with two escorts who carried my luggage. She told me my father had instructed that I be treated like a prince. A young, petite and elegantly dressed woman with elfin features awaited. With a beautiful French accent, she introduced herself as Nancy and politely asked how my flight had been. I replied, with a slight and wary smile, that it was fine. She smiled as the stewardess handed her the paperwork on a clipboard to sign, then turned to me and said she should get me home. I nodded in acceptance, quietly thanked the stewardess, and followed Nancy. As we walked towards the exit, I tried to imagine what living in New York would be like and how soon I would be able to return home.

A vehicle awaited us as we exited the building. It was large and extremely regal. I remember thinking the air was, strangely, as humid as in Trinidad. A tall man in a black suit and hat stood with the back passenger door open. I followed Nancy into the car. The driver closed the door, assisted the escorts with my luggage then proceeded to drive us to my new home. Throughout the journey, I stared out of the windows with curiosity as the view changed numerous times, from being on a highway to crossing an amazing bridge, huge towering buildings to townhouses on my right and a very large park on my left. My father had taken me to many countries and cities but we had never visited New York. I knew it was his home but it had never bothered me that we had not been there before. Right then, as we drove through this unfamiliar cityscape, I wished I had some previous memories of this place to cling to. I asked Nancy what type of car we were travelling in.

'It's a Bentley Sedanca de Ville and it belongs to you – well, your father.'

'What do you mean?'

She smiled at me, then whispered that we had arrived. The car stopped in front of a large ornate building. The driver got out and opened the passenger door for us. Nancy walked up the front steps with me close behind her, while the driver followed with my luggage. The front door was already open and a woman stood waiting as if we were at a hotel. As we entered the luxuriously decorated foyer I was amazed, but did not show it. An elaborate chandelier and the grand staircase did distract me for a brief moment though.

'Welcome home,' Nancy said.

'Is this your home, too?'

She looked at me and softly replied, 'This is your father's home, and your home now.'

With that said, she insisted on showing me to my room so I could settle in and promised to give me a tour of the house the following day. We went up two flights of stairs and along a huge corridor before stopping at a door.

'This is my room. If you need anything, no matter what the time, don't be afraid to come find me.' She continued down the corridor to the next door. 'This is your bedroom.'

She kindly suggested that I make myself at home, turned and left. I stood there for a moment. This mysterious, enormous place was so alien to me and I felt overwhelmed with the tornado of events that had landed me there. I cautiously opened the door. When I entered the room I was taken aback; it had been designed to look exactly like my bedroom in Trinidad. I felt a wave of warm relief. I guess my dad, in his own way, really was trying to make sure I felt safe and comfortable. It worked. I jumped onto the big soft bed and fell into a deep, dreamless sleep, still fully clothed, with my favourite pair of Chucks still on my feet.

I awoke, confused initially as to my location, both familiar and foreign, to the sound of loud calypso music. I knew the song well; it was by the calypsonian Aldric Farrell. Popularity had earned him the moniker, "The Boy Wonder", though some time after he reverted to "Pretender", a previous nickname from his school days. The song playing was '*Ode to the Negro Race*' and it was one of Maria's and my favourites. I bounced out of bed and with memories flooding back of dancing in the kitchen with Maria, I left my bedroom and followed the music, rubbing my eyes. It led to a big welcoming kitchen where I found Nancy singing the chorus, '*God made us all and in 'em we trust, so nobody in de world is better dan us.*'

'Apt, isn't it,' was her greeting. I must have looked puzzled. 'The song. We're all equal.'

She was sitting at a breakfast bar and the woman I passed at the main door the night before was serving her breakfast. Together they asked if I slept okay. I responded with an uncertain smile as Nancy introduced me to the woman.

'This is Gertrude, she's our housekeeper and the gentleman who brought us home last night is Ian, he's our butler and will also be your chauffeur.'

'My chauffeur? Why do I need a chauffeur?'

'New York City is a lot bigger, more diverse and at times more dangerous than Trinidad, so you will not be able to get to high school on your own after the summer is over. Besides, you will also need Ian to take you to your doctor's appointments.' She paused for a moment, thinking.

'I'll take you to your first appointment, later on today.'

'Why do I need a doctor? No one has told me yet.'

'I'm not entirely sure,' Nancy replied, tilting her head and reaching for my arm. 'He's a therapist and I assume it's because of the hallucinations you suffered a few days ago,' her expression warm. 'It's your father's orders and luckily he is a very wealthy, influential man with the ability to get you the treatment you require so quickly and with the best physician. I'm sure the doctor will look after you wonderfully.'

'My father, a wealthy and influential man?' I asked, frowning.

'Yes, I guess he's considered to be an oil tycoon.' She looked at me, puzzled. 'Did you not know?'

I actually did not know exactly what my father did, nor had I ever asked. We lived a pleasant life and I was too young and carefree to think about the adult world of work.

'He works for a private organisation in the oil industry, in Trinidad, doesn't he?' I asked.

Nancy explained how that was partially the truth; that he had a number of organisations within the oil industry, the newest founded in Trinidad with the aim to pioneer the use of natural gas as a chemical feedstock in the manufacturing of ammonia. I had no idea what all of that meant and talking about my dad was making me miss him more.

'What do you do for him?'

She smiled enigmatically.

'I have worked for your father for the past seventeen years as his personal assistant but I would like to think that we are great friends now. Come, let's show you around your new home.' Off she went and I followed behind her, full of curiosity. I had warmed to her and surprisingly, was already beginning to feel a little more relaxed, although not quite settled.

The house was extremely large, with many facilities including a swimming pool and indoor tennis court, which Nancy informed me would also be used for my fencing lessons. I was over-awed and fascinated; it seemed like a new life here had been created for me overnight.

'So, what would you like to do?' she asked.

'I'm a bit hungry, and later, I might like a swim.'

We walked back to the kitchen where we found Gertrude, still swaying her ample hips to the calypso music. She greeted me warmly and asked what juice I would like.

'Mango, please,' I replied as I sat at the table. She brought over a carafe prepared from the produce my father had sent with me, poured me a glassful then placed a serviette on my lap. Shortly after, she served me a big pile of pancakes with fruit and cream. She ruffled my hair and said that I was just like my father. I felt then that Gertrude and I would become good friends, although a pang of homesickness and longing for Maria trailed as well. As though reading my mind, Gertrude pulled up the chair next to me and scooped me into a big motherly hug.

'It's okay, darling, we'll take great care of you. Never ever worry.'

Reunion

Later that afternoon, after much exploration of the house and a fun swim in the pool, Nancy drove me to my doctor's appointment in the most beautiful cabriolet I had ever seen. She told me it was a Mark IV. 'Without the S.S. badge,' she quickly added. I did not know what she meant but I can clearly remember how mesmerised I was by the shiny, sprinting cat perched on the nose of the bonnet. The car was a gift to her from my father for looking after me, and the new love of her life, she told me with a chuckle. The sound, smell and feeling of acceleration in this car would go on to fuel my love of fast cars, power yachts and jets throughout my adult life.

We drove down 5th Avenue, made a right onto 42nd Street and continued turning left, making a large semicircle around a beautiful city park, eventually pulling over on the right side of West 40th Street in front of an impressive dark brick building: it was as dark as coal with gold brick accents glistening in the sunlight. I looked at Nancy, unease visible on my face as she pointed towards a small townhouse to the side of the ornate American Radiator edifice, as I now know it to be. Nancy informed me the smaller structure she was pointing out was the home of my therapist. An intimidating black door with a large metal door knocker sat prominently in a white facade. I reluctantly got out of the car and stood on the sidewalk, looking around.

'I'll be right here when you come out,' Nancy said.

The sidewalk was clean, the air filled with a mixture of aromas. The most noticeable was that of the blossoming flowers across the street in the busy park. People walked by, going about their business; they looked relaxed and happy. Some appeared to be in a bit of a rush but only their brisk walks gave them away. The men were dressed in sharp suits, the women looked immaculately groomed, many wearing bright red lipstick.

I walked along the sidewalk and reached for the door knocker, looking back at Nancy who was waiting to see that I was safely inside. The door opened and a young, well-groomed man wearing glasses, in a beautifully fitted double-breasted suit, greeted me. He was showing out another boy who looked to be about my age and a woman who I guessed must have been his mother.

'You must be Kairi, my three thirty appointment. This is Stanley and Adele, and I'm Timothy.'

The woman smiled politely at me as Timothy reached down to shake my small hand. The boy barely looked at me. Little did we know we would grow up to become close friends. I cautiously entered as he bid them goodbye and they left. He closed the door and gestured with his hand for me to follow him.

'I like your home.' It was the only thing I could think of saying at the time.

'Me, too. It has its own identity. In the shadows of the gothic, castle-like structure next door, it's almost invisible. In the park right across the street, I can have a game of chess in the mornings with my coffee. It can be dull at times but overall, the perfect area for my research on exploring the therapeutic potential of psychedelic drugs under controlled conditions.'

I had no idea what he was talking about. He kept looking back at me as I followed him to what I presumed was his office, a small but bright room thanks to the large, wooden, double-hung sash window to the back of the property. He sat on a leather chair in the corner of the room and asked me to make myself comfortable on a leather chaise longue under the dominating window.

I expected him to delve straight into the topic of what I had seen back in Trinidad but instead, he told me a little about himself. I listened, uninterested, looking out of the window until he asked me to tell him about myself.

'How are you going to help me?' I enquired, now somewhat more inquisitive.

'That's not exactly my aim. I'm going to encourage you to help yourself.'

This left me even more confused, but now, looking back, I think it was intentional. I hesitated, then conceded with honesty.

We discussed many things during my weekly visits and I began looking forward to seeing him. We had talked about me starting my new school and before I knew it, I was in my torturously smart uniform, walking through the grand gates of the private school I had been placed into.

I spoke to my father over the telephone every now and again but not as frequently as I would have liked. My conversations with Maria had also petered off as I grew closer to Gertrude and Nancy and shared my feelings and anxieties with Tim.

That period of calm in my life did not last. The disturbing news of my father's murder would change everything once more. I remember feeling numb and everyone constantly asking if I was okay. I would coldly reply, 'Yes,' every time I was asked. I felt guilty for not crying but when I tried to cry no tears came, just a strange hollow feeling. Thankfully, I was protected from the grisly details of his death until I was deemed old enough to bear them.

My father had been missing for thirteen days before he was found murdered, decapitated, in the local cemetery in Fyzabad, his mutilated body found at my mother's crypt and no one had any clues as to what had happened. Oddly, there was no blood at the crime scene, insinuating he had been deposited there *after* his tragic demise. They discovered later that the wound had been cauterised. Due to my father's importance, the local police flew in crime scene investigators from both Scotland Yard and the United States but no one could identify the method of decapitation, nor any motive for the severe transgression. The evidence, or lack of and the strangeness of the crime made it even more mysterious.

'*It appears his head was pulled from his body by something with the power of ten men,*' the coroner wrote. The cemetery he was found in was an unsafe and overgrown, dreary place, rumoured as the prime location for practising *Obeah* in the village. This caused a lot of speculation and rumours by the locals, I was told, many years later.

When my mother died my father had a large white stone crypt built, the area protected with high walls overgrown with all manner of wild vines. A beautifully designed wrought-iron gate and locks secured its safety and our privacy when we visited her, but also prevented grave robbers. He had told me how people would disturb the resting place of the dead just to steal their expensive coffins, only to sell them to unsuspecting individuals trying to give their deceased relatives a respectable send-off.

While growing up in Fyzabad my friends and their families all thought my mother's crypt was elaborate but I loved going there to visit her and they had no idea of the magical place that lay out of sight, beyond the gates. The gravel walkway was lined with a mixture of poui trees, giving an array of blossoms in my mother's favourite colours, and gently swayed in the tropical breezes all year round. The entire crypt was covered in a green vine with a small white flower that smelt divine. I think my father called it Jasminum sambac; he said my mother loved the flower's scent. Even now, when I walk in a garden and smell that unusual flower, I am overwhelmed with sweet memories and sadness for that little boy who lost his parents far too soon.

Kai looked as though he would begin to cry at any moment. I was worried and it was getting late but I couldn't stop him, I really wanted to know more. Gently wiping his eyes, he continued.

We would enter the gateway, then go down the stone staircase, lit by burning torches that I always assumed the old caretaker at the cemetery kept alight for us. The staircase led to another wrought-iron gate, leading into a chamber with a vaulted ceiling adorned with painted blossoms mirroring the flowers of the trees outside. The stone walls were decorated with intricate carvings of local animals: iguanas, agoutis, fauns, and silky anteaters – locally referred to as pomeyones. My mother lay in the centre of the room, within a stone chamber painted with the same blossoms as the vaulted ceiling.

It pained me to know that this place of peace and beauty where I could mourn my mother had been tarnished so grotesquely by the brutal murder of my father. My father's head was never recovered and the rest of his body, after a lengthy investigation, was entombed with the remains of my mother in her final resting place. This pain was mixed with relief that my father came to rest alongside my mother as he had always wanted. It was a strange time and although it feels uncomfortable to admit it, once the numbness had worn off, I felt oddly comforted to know that they were finally reunited and neither of them would be lonely any more.

I had grown into a tenacious, independent young man and as promised, my father had left me in good hands with Nancy and Gertrude, and with such a vast fortune, it seemed I would always be okay.

Gang Gang Sarah

Many years had now passed. It was 1977, I was a forty-four-year-old socialite still living in New York City. I had been counting down the days of the week and although I was both nervous and excited, the weekend could not come quickly enough. It was planned to perfection, with no expense spared. Finally, Friday had arrived. It was around midday and the chauffeur drove the customised phantom black, imported European, V8 powered four-by-four uptown towards my girlfriend Marita's East Side apartment, while I sat comfortably reclined, looking completely in control but perspiring slightly.

We had been dating for just over two years. It was my first monogamous relationship and I was about to take her on holiday. It was not the first time we had been away together but it was going to be Marita's first visit to Trinidad and Tobago. It was also the first time I was returning since my father's funeral. I had been to the Caribbean many times since, but not Trinidad and Tobago. Despite being together for some time, Marita felt she did not know much about my early years growing up there; it was a period of my life I was not sure how to share, but seeing that this was the woman I wanted to spend the rest of my life with, I decided to share it *all* and while there, I was going to ask her to marry me.

She was smart, strong and kind, caring more for others than I did and certainly more environmentally conscious than I was, she really did care about the welfare of our planet. Marita hated the refined four-by-four I was ferried around in, "Gas guzzler", she labelled it. I could not disagree, I was lucky if it drove ten miles on a single gallon of fuel; not that I cared about the running cost of the luxurious vehicle, but I think my ignorance infuriated Marita even more. She reminded me on numerous occasions that change could occur from just one person at a time and implored me to improve on my over-consumption of fuel.

'It would be one more person in the world practising obsolescence of something harmful to our planet,' she would say.

She was not naive and understood the necessity of fuel – the internal combustion engine and catalytic converters – but her argument was valid and she would suggest I take the subway as much as I could to lower my personal toxic gas emissions. At first, because I did not care much nor in truth, pay the environment the respect it is truly due, I ignored her. Over time I began realising what was at stake, our fundamental right to inhale clean, breathable, oxygenated air. Our moral duty to protect plants, animals and our environment as a whole for our children and generations thereafter. We cannot continue to treat other species and our own in the manner we have previously, such as the already forgotten and almost mythical dodo, its demise no fault of its own but instead humanity's greed and aching need to devour all.

Marita's reasoning grew on me: knowledgeable and passionate about the cause, she was certainly inspirational. She would point out how the National Geographic Society have been continuously trying since 1888 to inspire people to care for our planet. I needed to change my gas guzzlers after returning from this trip, I nervously thought.

As a society at that time, we really did not understand much about our carbon footprint and sadly, although the US government had already, in 1955, established funding schemes to aid research into air pollution, the role of this egalitarian government was still limited. Large firms hid, manipulated and green-washed the truth of their products, oil and its by-products, which only fed society's unquenchable consumption, forcing our planet into a catastrophic state of global warming. Nevertheless, we continued to march on with our heads raised to the clouds of naivety.

We arrived at Marita's apartment building and she was already in the lobby, eagerly waiting. The doorman opened the entrance doors and began loading her luggage into the large boot. Ian opened the passenger door of the vehicle for her. She hopped in with an informal kick and threw herself into my lap with the warmest of kisses. I loved her greetings.

Thinking back now, neither of us were wearing our seatbelts. The law in New York did not require us to wear those uncomfortable harnesses until 1984. It is sad that our stupidity needed a law to force us to wear a device that has saved numerous lives to this day.

Marita stayed like a cat, curled up in my lap, chatting to me while Ian drove us to JFK airport. Her nickname was "Kitty", Marita Kitty Jay is what I affectionately called her. To me she was perfect, her presence could transfix me like a rabbit in headlights. Her large Picasso eyes, bottomless pools of honey on her lustrous skin, saw beauty in everything. Her nose dainty, lips delicate but deliciously plump, and her hair, long sumptuous dark curls cascading over her slender bronzed shoulders, her physique exquisite. She had the power to turn everything I was accustomed to upside down.

Before we knew it we had arrived and we were boarding our aircraft. Makeeda, our stewardess, welcomed us aboard while Michael and Brian, my two pilots, had already completed their pre-flight checks and were in the cockpit, ready to depart. I was excited; we were about to travel in my new Learjet 25D, I had not seen it before now. The outside had a beautiful two-toned paint job, the top a matte gold and the bottom navy blue with a silver accent dividing the two colours. The cabin was designed with usable spaces, a fitted kitchen and water closet furnished with high gloss rosewood veneer cabinets dividing the cockpit and main cabin. The interior was custom finished with navy blue carpets and white leather paneling. In the cockpit there were six white leather seats with high gloss rosewood inlays. I was very pleased with my new purchase.

'I feel guilty for loving it,' Marita swooned as she looked around the cabin.

I went to say hello to the pilots, eager to share in their excitement over our new toy and as I expected, they were ecstatic. My on-board flight staff had all been with me for over five years and we were all pretty close, with a relaxed relationship filled with trust. Their service provided was essential as I had already experienced too many near misses and now preferred someone else in the driver's seat. Through Nancy's influence, I had become somewhat of a thrill seeker.

After settling in, we took off at once, heading for Crown Point Airstrip in Tobago. It was a very comfortable flight but my excitement began to evaporate as I now felt slightly worried; feelings I had expected, I guess. Marita was aware my parents had died but did not know any of the details and I had promised myself to be less vague with her about that period of my life.

After hours of relaxation and being pampered we began our descent at Crown Point. I could see the smile on Marita's face, she was enjoying the view of Buccoo Reef. I had forgotten how hypnotizingly beautiful the coral reef was.

It was a smooth landing; the jet gently manoeuvred into our private hanger where two more phantom black gas guzzlers, unmanned, with the keys in the ignition, awaited us. We all helped and quickly transferred our luggage from the jet to the four-by-fours and set off again, driving up-island towards Castara Bay, Michael, Brian and Makeeda following behind us.

'What's the plan?' Marita asked with a suspicious smile.

'It's a surprise,' I replied.

Our road trip took us through a small village named Les Coteaux. I told Marita I could remember driving through here with my father and she gently stroked my thigh. In the village stood a creepy old timber church, in front of which sat an elderly woman selling little posies of wild flowers. Further down the street a younger woman stood next to a makeshift table, selling handmade jewellery. Marita wanted to stop and we did. While she and Makeeda, who had quickly joined her, admired the young woman's creations I stood looking around the village surprised at how much it had not changed since I was last there. I walked up towards the lady with the flowers; she had just three posies of yellow, pink and white Jasmine left. Surprised that they were Jasminum Sambac, I asked how much.

'*Ten TT,*' she replied with a strong Tobagonian accent.

I gave her fifty US dollars, two twenties and a ten, took all three posies, thanked her and walked back over towards Marita and Makeeda. They each took a posy, leaving me the pink one and chuckling with each other at me absent-mindedly smelling my pretty pink flowers. They both chose a few pieces of jewellery, I paid the young woman for them and we began walking back to our vehicles. The old flower woman followed, walking up to me and placing a leather necklace around my neck with a sharp, pitted, glass-like shard pendant attached to it.

'*Obsidian,*' she said, '*or as we folk call it, "Devil's Fire".*'

Although a little surprised by her actions I did not pull away. Instead I asked, 'How much?'

'*It doh cost nutten and it might jus' protect yuh.*'

I smiled politely, thanking her so as not to offend her generosity. Then, she told me her name was Gang Gang Sarah and that Ms Hilda, in keeping with her promise, had asked her to look after me. I was of course stunned. Seeing the puzzled look on my face as I got back into the vehicle, Marita asked, 'Who was that?'

'Someone from my past, I guess.' I drove off feeling unsettled, pondering what had just happened.

We were not far now from Cotton Bay and I could not wait to get there. I decided to myself that we would not stay in this peculiar land for any longer than we had to, reminding myself to stay out of the forest.

The winding roads took us through our journey without any detours. As we approached our destination we slowed and waited for the electric gates to open, granting us entry. We drove up the manicured driveway lined with burning fire pits and carved marble statues, towards what looked like a stone pagoda manned with two people who were waiting for us. I could see Marita was both fascinated and intrigued. As we stopped, a young groomed Rastafarian man opened Marita's door, seeing her safely out of the vehicle, then went to aid his companion with unloading the luggage.

Beyond the pagoda, looking downwards, was a stone jetty, lined with more softly burning fire pits, stretching into the sky-blue Caribbean waters against an array of pinks and blues as the looming sunset approached. A large gold and navy blue yacht was moored at the end of the jetty, glistening against the vibrant night-shining sky. *Themistocles*, a hundred and seventy-three-foot triple deck yacht with a maximum speed of sixteen knots, finished three months previously by a naval architect in Italy. This was going to be our temporary home while we vacationed in the Caribbean. Island hopping, as my personal assistant had called the trip.

With our arms wrapped around each other's waists, we walked down the jetty towards the prepossessing vessel. It seemed strangely silent on board and Marita asked where the crew were. Before I could reply, all her family and a handful of our dearest friends jumped out, all shouting, 'Surprise!' Marita could not believe it.

'Why are you all here?' she asked, laughing. I lowered myself to one knee.

'I wanted to ask you a question and thought it would be better to have everyone here to *hopefully* celebrate afterwards.'

By now she had her hands over her mouth and her large hazel-brown eyes became glossy. I smiled at her, surprisingly nervous, taking the ring out of my pocket.

'Will you marry me?'

She offered her hand and I placed the unique, custom made ring on her finger, then she gently held my face and whispered, 'Yes,' into my ear before softly and tenderly kissing my cheek. As she kissed my lips I remember hearing everyone cheering and the popping sounds of champagne bottles. Everyone seemed so happy for us.

The crew appeared and we cast off, leaving Tobago's picturesqueness behind us and making our way to Trinidad. After mingling with everyone Marita and I left our guests happily enjoying the celebrations, while we sought out a quiet spot to enjoy the now darker sky. Marita walked, still swaying her hips to the music blaring in the distance. Armed with a bottle of champagne and two glasses we settled down alone on a sun bed on the bow of the yacht. Warmly contented we relaxed, quietly enjoying the calm seas, communicating with loving glances, soft strokes and kisses that promised our future happiness.

'I swear the stone on my ring has changed colour,' she said with her left hand held up, inspecting her new black fascination adorned with the distinctive gemstone.

'It has,' I responded with a confident smile. I had been practising the following speech almost as long as when I first decided to propose.

'The stone was found in the mountains of Brazil, precious and rare, not quite as yourself but you know what I mean,' I added, still beaming at her. 'Its an alexandrite. As you know, a growing number of illegal miners have been operating within the Amazon rainforest, causing environmental damage and disruption of the indigenous tribes living on what is supposed to be protected land. One tribe, in particular, have faced huge problems caused by illnesses introduced by the illegal miners. Almost half the inhabitants have died from diseases which they encountered for the first time.

'Although my mineral mine was not in the same vicinity, we had to help. We intervened, aided by the government and took in a team of anthropologists and doctors with the necessary medicines. After helping as much as we could – well, as much as they would let us – we warned them of the greed of man.

'Your ring has been hand crafted with twenty-four carat gold from my mine, the production process manipulated using black rhodium to give it its black colour. The gold was cultivated in a more ethical manner than in most other mining operations, transparent and sustainable without machines or intensive labour, nor any harm to the rainforest. The alexandrite gemstone is a hundred and sixty-three carats, a split-ended keystone cut, red and green in colour, depending on the light. A genuine gift from the Yapu people for helping. I could not refuse, it would have been disrespectful. Besides, I had strict instructions to use it to propose to you.'

Marita was speechless for a brief moment.

'Tell me more about the Yapu's. Can I meet them?'

'Probably. The likelihood of them needing further support seems almost certain,' I answered to her excited curiosity, causing her thrill to mutate into concern.

'The Yapu's are believed to be descendants of anacondas. Known as the Sons and Daughters of the Anacondas, they reside deep in the Amazon jungle, a thirty-nine-day walk or an eight-day river journey from the nearest civilisation.' Marita was staring with a gaping mouth.

'Yet still illegal miners found them,' she softly replied, disappointed. She paused, admiring her ring with an even deeper fascination.

'I adore my ring, how special.'

Duppies

The night sky was lit by an impressive moon and although still unable to resist each other, our focus was on the mesmerisingly beautiful array of stars which seemed almost close enough to pick. Trinidad began materialising in the distance, a bay visible with the aid of the bright night sky and a large flame. I was not sure exactly which bay it was, but I was certain we were on the northern coast of the island.

The beach in the distance was dominated by a large bonfire, the crackling light displaying what appeared to be people dancing around it. Both curious, we stood up, trying to see what was going on. Almost instantaneously, from nowhere a curtain of fog engulfed *Themistocles*. It made no sense, the immediateness of the fog's appearance and potency should be impossible. We grabbed hold of each other and I can remember with great clarity the sound of Marita's voice saying she was scared. I looked back along the yacht as I realised the music and voices from our guests were now gone. I could only see the dirty haar, it was cold and weighted. A queer, frightful feeling rushed upon me from deep within my subconscious, the memories and emotions of the night I encountered the douens in the forest fully returned.

As quickly as the fog appeared it vanished. We were a lot closer to the beach now and everything was more visible. The bonfire dancers looked primitive. Clutching spears and shields they danced, chanting an eerie incantational ritual while majestic male peacocks strutted around the beach freely.

About fifty yards away from the group and separated by a row of canoes were two more figures. Next to them were three spears augured into the ground, the tops tied together, taking shape like a tipi, hanging a cauldron above a smaller bonfire. Of the two figures, one was an unclothed female bound to what appeared to be a totem pole, her pleading screams travelling crisply over the water. The other individual looked like a chief or cacique, wearing a large peacock feathered headpiece and garments different from the others. He stood above the cauldron stirring it with a large wooden staff, occasionally belabouring the girl with the smouldering stick then losing himself in his dance ritual.

Pulling Marita with me I ran towards the middle deck. None of our friends or family were there. No one was there. We ran to the helm on the top deck with the intention of stopping the yacht, still steadily en route for that strange beach with no sign of slowing down, but all the sophisticated equipment needed to steer the yacht was destroyed. We stood for a second in disbelief and with no time to think *Themistocles* ran aground, throwing us down violently. Both conscious and without any major injuries. I helped Marita off the ground and we rushed to hide.

The sounds of chanting and splashing water were ominously closer now and we feared these strange people were boarding the vessel. We climbed out of an escape hatch leading to the top of the yacht, closed it behind us and lay on the hatch to stop anyone else trying to follow. There was no other way to get up there so we felt momentarily safer. We lay completely still and silent and could hear the rustling sounds of the spirit of curiosity aboard the yacht. Adding to my disquiet was the reverberating pulse of Marita's heartbeat. My face, neck and body were wet from sweat, my heart heavily thumping to the sound of the ticking hands of my Audemars Piguet embracing my wrist. It was given to me five years previously by Timothy as a more efficient means of time keeping as I was now self-medicating. Oddly, the phantoms sounded uninterested, and eventually left; we could see them all heading back to the beach, returning to their chanting and ritualistic behaviour. It did not sound like they had found anyone else below deck. We waited until they were preoccupied with their activities, then opened the hatch and climbed back down into the cockpit. From there, with our almost matching, his-and-hers loafers in hand, we stealthily climbed down the quarterdeck, headed towards the aft and quietly went over the side into the shallow warm tropical waters. The dark shadow of the yacht gave us cover to take a minute and assess our next move while still observing what was occurring on the mysterious beach. We counted to make sure all thirteen individuals were now back on the beach and not planning a surprise trap on us. The chief had gone back to terrorising his captive, we could hear the sound of her skin sizzling each time he hit her with his burning staff, it was unbearable but there was nothing we could do to help. The rest of the tribe seemed to be wrestling or fighting with one another, accompanied by their chants.

While treading water, a white hummingbird appeared, flying around our heads. The fragile creature darted around us repeatedly, then came to a halt and began hovering upside down like a playful dolphin, it seemed, as if trying to get our attention. This was to be the first of my encounters with this little spirit-like creature.

'Follow me.' It was the faintest of voices, delicate and feminine, barely to be heard but clearly came from the tiny creature. Marita and I looked at each other, startled, then it flew off in the direction of the beach not too far away, goading us forward. We were not as hesitant as one might expect and hurriedly followed the little bird, capitalising on the current distraction of the altercation amongst the natives and before losing what could be our last opportunity to escape. Marita and I noiselessly waded out of the warm sea and snuck up onto the sandy beach. We followed the hummingbird and made our way through the canoes, towards a canopy of coconut trees and bushes backing off the beach, the soft cool sand clinging to our wet ankles and feet. Fuelled with adrenaline, shoes still in hand, unafraid of potential prickles, we cautiously but hastily followed the winged creature deeper into the forest. It was not uncomfortably dark but still the last place either of us wanted to be: better here though, than being devoured by what appeared to be painted cannibals.

We were both certainly bemused and stunned by what had just transpired. Where had everyone vanished to on the yacht? Why were there savage Carib-like Indians on a beach in Trinidad? They should be extinct except maybe distant relatives, but then, we were following a talking bird. I must be dreaming.

Keeping Marita in front of me, our fear kept us moving quickly. We arrived at a sudden left turn on the pathway. The hummingbird took the sharp corner without pausing and we followed, but as we broke the corner the unusual creature evaporated into a puff of smoke. Marita stopped abruptly; I unintentionally skated into the back of her with a thump; she jolted. 'Ay!' she exclaimed.

We had been brought to an old wooden open gateway or entrance and could see that there was a person standing directly in front of us. Uncertain what to do next, it immediately felt like a Mexican stand-off. As though by magic, two grounded flambeaux ignited, made from stout rum bottles, lighting the entrance and both sides of the now visibly tall, dark, male body. Adorned in black, he wore the strangest clothes; a shimmery shirt, bell bottom trousers, leather boots and a wide-brimmed hat with white caskets roughly painted on the crown. Most importantly, he had a pistol in his right hand and a strange club tipped with a solid coffin-like shape in the other. It would not have been a good idea to try to run.

'I am de Midnight Robber. Follow meh.'

He turned around in a choleric manner, almost robotic but with a familiar cowboy flair, walking through the gateway and down a narrow dirt road towards what resembled a hamlet, his flowing cape embellished with white brush strokes in the form of a skull and crucifix. With little choice in the matter, we hurriedly put on our shoes and reluctantly followed. At every indecisive step more flambeaux ignited, strangely synchronised, lighting two at a time as our bodies ploddingly paced past them, making our way visible. There were so many of them, they must have been recycled rum bottles left behind by the pirates of yesteryear. The smell of burning kerosene was now strong in the air, reminiscent of growing up in Fyzabad. Many of the villagers there did not have electricity and alternatively used homemade kerosene lamps, or pitch-oil lamps as we called them back then; they glowed just like the corpulent, flickering bottles did now.

We passed old timber buildings either side of the dirt road, some on wonky stilts up in the air, others flat on the ground like bungalows. Hints of calypso music travelled with the light wind every now and again, blotted with voices. Marita held tightly on to my hand. We walked for a few minutes more; this is what someone walking towards their execution must feel like. I was terrified and could only imagine how Marita must have been feeling. He stopped abruptly.

'*Yuh should be safe here fuh ah bit.*'

As he spoke, flambeaux began to ignite everywhere, running in continuous lines into the distance along the dirt road we were following and the perpendicularly visible road we now stood on. It was a junction, the glowing crossroads all lit up by the many flaming bottles. In this bizarrely beautiful setting I think we forgot our fear for a moment; similar to the Diwali celebrations when many Hindus use diyas to create lit-up shapes to celebrate the significance of light overcoming darkness. This peaceful beauty was short lived as a theatrical masquerade descended upon us. Many people appeared in every direction, bringing with them tables, chairs and even more flaming torches. A live band danced through, settling into position while playing. It was the strangest thing; they were like stage actors at a theatre.

A table was forced between Marita and me, a flambeau placed upon it and chairs pushed behind us, forcing us to sit opposite each other. I looked at the flambeau, now perfectly visible. "Mount Gay, Est. 1703, Barbados Rum Black Barrel", the words on the recycled bottle read. We were in the centre of the junction under a curious sky, with strange people in peculiar costumes all bustling around us. We glanced at each other, expressively shocked.

'Kai,' Marita whispered anxiously.

The Midnight Robber had gone and in his place, in command of this strange performance, a woman in white approached, cradling a baby in one arm and holding a circular tray with the other. The baby did not look real, nor alive, rather like a rotted cassava root. I was baffled. Marita had her hands over her mouth, demonstrating disgust.

'Is that baby dead!'

There was no response. The smell had me quiet; I felt uncontrollably nauseous and kept surreptitiously swallowing so as not to show my fear.

The woman's skin was dark but with an ashy tinge, long unbound dishevelled hair hanging over her face, her mouth and chin partially showing. On her tray were a sealed bottle of rum – the same bottle the flambeaux were all made from – two glasses and a green coconut which she slid onto a corner of the table. She stood there momentarily like a waitress. Without warning she dropped the dried-up fetus to the ground. Marita and I jumped. She placed a glass in front of each of us then calmly drew a machete from her sash. We both pulled back in our seats. Clenching the machete in one hand, she lifted the coconut with the other; a few quick chops and the nut was open, then she slid the machete back to where she had retrieved it from. Without a word she poured us both half a glass of coconut water, gently placing the coconut back on the tray, slightly tilted to protect the rest of the liquid in the nut; then she uncorked the golden rum, mixing both of our drinks with a generous amount before returning the bottle. The aroma of the rum, distinctively memorable but harbouring hints of spices, mysteriously indistinguishable. I was brought back to reality as she rubbed her hands together, stood over us smiling, looking left and right to us both, gesturing for us to drink.

Her teeth were all broken and ground into fangs, black and rotten. She crouched down and picked up the fetus. As she rose back up she looked at Marita.

'*Ah will take dat chile from yuh womb.*'

It was horrid. Blood sprayed out of her mouth, running down her chin as she spoke; then, storming off, she disappeared into the crowd.

'What the hell just happened?' Marita gasped.

'And what baby?' I asked nervously.

Only then it dawned on us the ruckus had stopped. We looked around intently. Everyone was dancing to the spiritous calypso music the band was performing. The scene around us was surreal; so many strange-looking characters, no one smiling and all dancing as though in a trance, moving their hips and waists in a winding motion;

wining, as all Caribbean people call that type of dancing. Maria came to mind, she used to *wine* the day away to calypso music while doing the house work. I missed her, she had died shortly after my father. She once told me that only *jamets* used to wine like that and how it never used to be acceptable behaviour for respectable folk, '*Buh thankfully times change*,' she would chuckle. I, of course, promptly asked her, 'What's a jamet?'

Maria was always honest and straightforward with me, she believed children were not to be mollycoddled and patronised but instead guided and treated like young adults, which was exactly how Maria saw me.

'*Ah jamet come from de patois word Diametre, meaning someone from de outer edges ah society, and in dis case, ah woman ah de night. Doh worry,*' she chuckled, '*When yuh grow up yuh'll learn all bout dem.*'

I was brought back to reality by the slamming of a chair at our table. An uncanny and distinguished old man sat down, placing his empty skull goblet on the table. This chalice was a fascinating piece of art, the base and stem made from dark pewter and ornate with images of different animals: agouti, wild boar, lappe and ocelot. The stem supported part of an upside-down skull, the occipital bone perfectly sawed towards the jaw leaving a bowl-like shape with teeth. Except for the maxilla, the rim of this drinking vessel was lined with more dark pewter and the sutures held in place by inky pewter pins. It was both macabre and beautiful, but surely it must leak, I thought. The old man was hairy, almost as you would imagine a werewolf to be. His skin as dark as night, he was tall and his body proportionately muscular with his face partially covered by a great moustache and beard. His nose appeared to have been broken on numerous occasions, the healing uneven, giving him a rugged facial appearance, yet his irregularly hairy face seemed kind. His only garment, a pair of once long, now tattered trousers, shredded to the knee and held on his hips by a belt of twisted vines with a bamboo horn hanging from it. His legs were like those of a great stag. The night could not have gotten any more preternatural.

'I am *Papa Bois*, and that strange woman who just left is a *churile*. She is very dangerous, mainly because you are pregnant,' he said, looking at Marita. He picked up the bottle of Black Barrel rum and helped himself, filling his goblet. 'This rum is excellent, it's my favourite, well, a favourite of many,' he said, gesturing towards the other tables around us, all holding bottles of the same delicious and intoxicating libation.

'How do you know I'm pregnant?' demanded Marita.

'We can all smell you, smell your baby.'

Marita looked at me, tears welling in her eyes.

'I'm sorry, I wanted to surprise you.' Crying, she placed her face in her hands. I leapt out of my chair and over to comfort her. I stood embracing her while she sat quietly for some time. We were both crying now; not only was I worried about our immediate safety but my paternal instinct kicked in and I was now severely concerned for our unborn child. My head spun to look at Papa Bois.

'What is a churile?'

'She is the spirit of a pregnant woman who died during childbirth,' he explained. 'Sometimes she may have committed suicide during pregnancy because of an injustice. Her eternal grief for the loss of her child can bring about, at times, misguided vengeance and when this happens a churile victimises pregnant women, whom she follows and possesses out of envy. Her violent attacks on women almost certainly cause miscarriages, even those who were closest to her in life are not safe from her retribution. She may also attack her former partner through the administering of illnesses, seeking revenge if he was cruel to her during their life, or if he had neglected or neglects the children she had successfully given birth to, for him, when she was human.' Papa Bois then turned, looking back at the crowd. 'These duppies, these shadowy spirits are a rare spectacle for the eyes of mortals. In actuality, you may be the first humans to witness these remnants of what were once descendants of the Bantu people.'

'Who are the Bantu people?' Marita exclaimed, her voice trembling at the realisation that these beings were apparitions.

'The term Bantu is an unprejudiced name, but depending on who you ask, can also be an offensive term for a vast ethnic group originally from the Central African region.' He sighed and took a drink from his goblet as he gathered his thoughts. 'Although ignored, they seem to be the only sensible ones within our civilisation. Fuelled with the honesty of not knowing, they believe in one supreme interpretation of God incorporating all its vagueness. To them God can be the surrounding nature, the sun at the centre of the solar system, or the black hole at the centre of our galaxy. I do not know how, but their beliefs have eradicated the ill frills religion can often bring with it.'

As Papa Bois elucidated, the crowd continued wining, only now their movements seemed more intense and vulgar. Tears mixed with sweat were rolling down their faces. Marita whispered in her native tongue, *'Ahora ellos están bailando con alma, como si hubieran sido poseídos por un duende.'* I understood what she meant: they were dancing with soul, as if possessed by fairies or goblin-like creatures, well known in Spanish mythology.

'The Devil's Breath!' Papa Bois shouted. 'They have consumed Devil's Breath,' he said again more softly.

'What is it?' Marita asked.

'A powerful drug derived from the seeds, flowers, and pollen of the borrachero tree—' but before he could continue, the familiar brume swiftly returned.

Enslavement

The action of making someone your possession.

The Fog

The same indistinct nebulous mass that had engulfed us aboard *Themistocles* plummeted down upon the already eerie little village, only this time, it seemed darker and just as before, began dispersing almost as quickly as it appeared. Instead of completely clearing, the queerest of things occurred: all the flambeaux went out simultaneously, the music stopped and everyone seemed scared. There was a lot of fidgety twittering, then silence. Hovering above our table, a dirt-covered female leg began climbing out of a lingering cloud. Another leg emerged, hairy with a cloven hoof, just like Papa Bois' but instead it was smouldering; glowing lava dripped from the sole, scorching the table. The body of a bewitching Melato woman followed.

'Ayiti!' Papa Bois shouted as he stood. 'You are not welcome here.'

Without hesitation, the fictitious woman, using her cloven hoof, kicked him in his chest. He and his chair lifted off the ground with great force, flying into the crowd of misfits, knocking over many. He was unconscious, and no longer helpful. She turned and with the back of her hand slapped me to the ground, tearing me from Marita's terrified clutch. As soon as I landed she leapt off the table. Her hoof dug into the dirt as she stood towering above me. She was not a large woman, just abnormally strong. She bent over and grabbed hold of me by my neck. I grabbed her wrist with no effect. She picked me up as though I were weightless, holding me in the air above her as high as her outstretched arm could reach. I felt insignificant.

Her hair was long with thick white curls covering one side of her face; her eyes a dirty-red, burning incandescently, as piercing as the devil's himself, one visibly clear as day, the other a faint glow through her chalky hair. Something was not entirely right with her face; the side her hair covered seemed disfigured. A blood-curdling shriek followed.

'I shall keep my prize safe until you return.'

She forced me to look over into the darkness. One flambeau lying on its side, still lit, showed me Marita on the ground fighting and kicking, bound by many of those faceless creatures I came to fear in my childhood. Unable to break free, Marita began screaming, piercing screams like the screech of an owl in the dead of night. I felt helpless and totally emasculated. I surrendered; both Ayiti and I knew that could be the only outcome.

'You have until the next full moon to deliver my body. If you fail, I will feed your delicate flower to my children.'

Her statement caused vexation to surge within me and with all my might I tugged on the stone shard hanging from my neck, gripping it to the point where it was cutting into my palm. I swung down with great force towards the chest of the tantalisingly, supercilious siren. It punctured her skin below her collarbone; she didn't budge. Her invincibility tolerated a slight glare down to the makeshift weapon. She dropped me to the ground before pulling out the stone blade from above her left breast, where a small, seemingly insignificant wound remained, leaving behind fragments of stone. Suddenly, like an erupting volcano, blood began gushing out of her flesh from beneath her beautiful caramel, but abnormally translucent, skin. Her revealing white blouse now covered in blood, she turned and smirked at me still lying on the ground, then unceremoniously, she stepped over me and walked towards Marita. The one flambeau went out.

In the darkness, I could hear the douens dragging Marita away, with Ayiti's hoof thudding the ground, following behind them. Marita never stopped screaming my name, growing fainter and fainter while I lay there, pathetic and sobbing hopelessly. As her screams faded they were replaced with the head-splitting night chorus of cicadas – tree crickets.

A few still moments, then the flambeaux all reignited. I slowly stood up; they were gone. Everyone was gone, except for Papa Bois. Still unconscious, he was the only other person, creature, still there. I went over to him but could not wake him, he wasn't breathing, I placed my ear on his chest; silence. Still snivelling, I thumped his chest out of hopeless anger. I stared at him for a moment, lying there on the ground amongst the broken tables and chairs then I picked myself up, turned and headed back the way we had come earlier.

I stumbled about, devastated at my inability to prevent Marita's kidnapping, slowly following the route back to the beach. Crouched, hiding in the bushes, I surveyed my surroundings. I could still distinguish the two bonfires, now just glowing embers and smoke; the young sacrificial woman still tied to the pole, motionless. I remained out of sight, concealed by the thick vegetation, patiently waiting on the impending daybreak. I could finally think, or at least try. Where was I? This could not be Trinidad—well, at least not the Trinidad I knew. I was aware the country was in a depression but still, torture, kidnappings and ritualistic drug use? I certainly was not expecting any of this. This country was, no, *is* a paradise.

When *Themistocles* passed through the fog it must have taken us somewhere else. Was that even possible? What was I thinking? Clearly, I was not thinking straight. I was distraught, sleep deprived and so thirsty, even hungry, I could not ignore that fact; my stomach noisily remindful.

Dawn arrived. Peacocks and their loud calls roamed the beach. A single canoe remained: it was different from the others that had been there before, it was longer. I felt uneasy and stayed hidden a while, fearful it was a trap, but nothing happened. Startled by the sudden appearance of my tiny defender, it was Silver, the white hummingbird that had tried to help us before. She flew around me numerous times, then stopped, hovering in front of me at face level.

'I brought help,' she said in her otherworldly, sprite-like voice. The creature then darted off over the beach, stopping above the strange canoe and hovering as though she wanted me to follow. Cautiously walking towards the canoe, I could not take my gaze away from the corpse on the pole. She was severely mangled and burnt, vital pieces were missing and what remained of her was held together now by the vines used to bound her upright to that foul pillar and by her own raw ligaments and stretched tissue clinging to many dismembered parts.

'F@#king savages!'

I walked infuriated over to my winged companion. My yacht was close by, right where we'd left it. It was a ghost ship, a *Mary Celeste*, with no sign or sound of anyone aboard. I dared not look at it for too long, aground without the crew or any of the guests: all missing, possibly dead.

'You must wait here, the prow of the longboat is not high enough to brave the sea.' With this advice she vanished, just as before.

I slumped onto the sand in front of the unusual longboat, confused but now fearless and filled with anger once more. I had lost everything that mattered to me. 'I must be cursed,' I said out loud. I felt a hand on my shoulder.

'What the—!' I flew up onto my feet, looking back alarmed. It was Papa Bois and the old woman from Tobago. I laughed nervously.

Kai sat up in his chair again, now looking at me more intently. 'It's funny how our minds work. Nervous, angry, scared, so many emotions within minutes of each other.'

I was still sitting on the floor of Kai's quiet little room in the care home in Plymouth, transfixed and unable to move.

'It is time for bed, we will catch up where we left off next weekend,' he said.

I was uneasy, somewhat scared and confused. My emotions were everywhere, just as Kai had described moments ago. As I stood I couldn't stop myself from shivering.

'Silver… that's what *you* call her?' I spluttered out of my quivering mouth.

'I know,' Kai said as he walked me out of his room. 'Goodnight.' He closed the door behind me.

I stood there, still, for some time. One of the care assistants caught my attention as she approached.

'I was just coming to check on you guys. It's late. Are you okay?'

'Yeah. Kai's okay also, he's just gone to bed.'

Looking at my watch, it was almost midnight. Dazed, I walked downstairs to the staff room, collected my things, said goodbye to the other staff members and left.

The walk home was surreal. I had my headphones in my ears but forgot to tap 'play' within my Tidal App. Shortly after, I arrived home to find Calvin there with some of our friends from China, all students but different majors. The smell of hotpot was in the air. It was late but because we were all from different countries, we had never really got over the time differences and time was never conventional to us. I went to my room and had a quick shower, trying to ignore what I'd learnt earlier and instead concentrate on the amazing smells coming from the lounge. I joined everyone to eat.

It was the perfect meal for a wintery spring night. The notion of hot-pot is as simple as it sounds: a basin-like pot on an electric portable burner, with a swirling divider in the centre of the pot to separate the yin and yang of the meal; two broths, one spicy, the other mild. Around the pot of simmering broths were plates, bowls, and plastic pots filled with mixed varieties of meats, seafood, tofu and vegetables. Chopsticks were tossed on the table amongst it all, the food ready to be cast into the boiling broth of your choice.

No two people in the group were from the same Chinese province, this was the main reason for the unusual mixture of ingredients. They explained to me that hotpot was different across Asia, the variations depended on location: in the southern parts people use predominantly fish; in the north, it's lamb; in the centre of the country or the Sichuan Province fiery ingredients are normally used. The larva-like spices help the 'See You Tomorrow,' one person added as she pointed to a bowl of strange mushrooms, making everyone erupt into laughter except myself—I didn't get the joke.

That's just in China, the rest of Asia is completely different. The only certainty is that hotpot is most enjoyable amongst family and friends who share a mutual respect. We were all gathered around the small square table, perched on chairs and stools. Calvin drew the short straw; he was perched on an upside-down bucket.

'How was your day?' one person asked me. I was so busy dipping my chopsticks into the delicious food that I couldn't even remember who asked, but I answered with a brief summary of the story I had just heard at the care home; not too much detail, nor who told me the tale, but it was enough to spark everyone's intrigue and we began sharing scary but fascinating stories.

One girl explained that sometimes when a person dies, if they have unfinished business, they may appear in a related person's dream and make requests, but these pleas are not always good. If the spirits are iniquitous it is believed that sometimes young children are able to see small, bloody footprints left behind as they go past. On other occasions the spirits can be even more sinister; the ghost can be malefic and possess its witness, making the child ill, eventually leading to death. If discovered, the unsympathetic you hun ye gui may directly harm the infant by strangulation or other violent means. She went on to tell us of a story she endured while growing up:

'I was only eight years old when a teacher at my school in China committed suicide. She jumped from the rooftop of the highest school building. As she fell the woman hit the bell tower, haemorrhaging, leaving a mess behind. When I arrived at the scene the body had already been removed but all the gore was still there. My peers at school would scare me, saying her sad soul would return to torment me and I feared this possible fate. To avoid these vengeful ghosts from returning, many believe gifts burnt will reach them in the afterlife and will fend off their ill-disposed behaviour. These gifts can be special gold or silver paper signifying money. Fruits, food and anything else that may please the deceased can work as well. One morning, after arriving at school I saw small bloody footprints in the girls' bathroom. I burnt anything I thought she would like, especially apples.'

Her own belief in her story made me confident; so much so, I wanted to share my own experiences but Calvin was staring at me. I knew what he meant. Men, we are like animals, we don't have to speak to each other to understand what we're thinking. I politely excused myself, pretending to be tired, and went directly off to bed.

In truth, I was partially tired and began thinking about my mom. She had always worked long hours to provide for my siblings and me when we were younger. Sadly, she still has to work just as hard now. My hope is to buy her a new home and look after her financially, so that she doesn't have to work any more.

Initially, when her marriage with my dad broke down, he left her with nothing. We didn't have a home and had no choice other than to stay at the homes of different relatives before eventually settling in with my mom's parents for a longer period. We lived there while my mom got her feet on the ground; it was not ideal but we were grateful. I knew we had nowhere else to turn to. My mom was a tough cookie, though, and she worked as many hours as she could. She found employment at a bakery for a while before settling into a more stable position with a security firm. It was around this time that my disappointing father gave her a small house for us to move into. I was young and my memories were muddled, but I think he was forced by the judicial system to give us that home.

The house was just a few feet away from my father's parents' home, still in the Saint Patrick county, in a town called Siparia. I think this was too close for comfort for my poor mom so she decided to sell it. Her mother and step-father had already given her a parcel of land next door to them in Fyzabad, where she hoped we could finally build a new home, something we all so deserved. The capital she had received for the sale of the previous house was not enough to build what we desired so she decided to join her funds with her brother and build a house we could all share. We were all so excited; no more sharing a double bed with three or sometimes four people.

The new build was to be a two-storey building: the upstairs, a three bedroom apartment belonging to my mom; the downstairs another three bedroom apartment to go to her brother, my uncle, whom we adored. They pooled their funds in an account and a few months later, when construction was to begin, the money was all gone. My uncle had stolen it all; her own brother. It was difficult for her to accept, *"E' would never do dat tuh meh,"* she kept saying. I can still remember how much she cried.

Some time went by, the pain of betrayal never leaving her eyes, but she continued to work hard and after a couple of years, she had saved a bit of money, enough for her to build the foundation for a small home on the vacant plot. A little time after that, we had walls, then a roof. It wasn't as beguiling as what she had previously planned for us, but it was a home. Without any funds remaining for windows or doors, we blocked up the holes in the walls with sheets of plywood and corrugated galvanized steel sheets. The front door was makeshift, part of a sheet of plywood on two hinges. It would swing open and shut when we required, giving us the dignity to be able to walk through that doorway and call our little space home.

For a short while we were completely fulfilled by what little we had. Sadly, it didn't last. My grandmother and step-grandfather would always remind us that it was they who gave us that plot of land; it was never a loving reminder but instead, always reproachful. The truth was, it was no one's land to give. We were all squatters: us, them, the neighbours; even the spooky long-mango tree that resided on the lot years before we did. They gave my siblings and me a complex. They were loving at times and we could always go over and get something to eat from my grandmother. I think they must have loved us. No matter what happened, I guess I knew I still loved them.

There was not much my tired mom could do now, and she really was tired. She would work twelve-hour night shifts with another three-hour commute added, and still somehow she would make it home most mornings to get us ready for school. She was exhausted whenever her head touched her pillow. I can vividly remember staying in and checking on her instead of playing in the garden with the other kids, it would scare me whenever I couldn't hear her breathing as she slept. Occasionally, when we wanted to play somewhere that we knew she would not allow, we would capitalise on the fact that she often talked in her sleep and would give us permission, oblivious to our schemes. When she figured out what we were doing, she passed a rule that no questions could be asked after she went to bed. She truly strived to make us feel safe in that unfinished structure – I lived there for about five years before leaving to go to America – and I really did feel safe, at least most of the time.

That same safe feeling sent me off to sleep.

Twenty-eighth ah May 2016

My anticipation was unbearable. I found it impossible to concentrate during my final week of deadlines and exams. Mercifully, Saturday finally arrived. After a brief conversation with my mom and siblings I left and went off to work. I was early. Today was my birthday and no one else here knew, except the one person I shared the date with. Awaiting my shift start, I took a cup of hot chocolate with me into the staff room and sat reading a newspaper. I had to be cautious; I didn't want my main purpose for being at work to be blatant to other members of staff. As my co-workers began pouring in to begin the day-shift, it transpired my team leader for that day was the care home owner who just happened to be the most fun and relaxed manager I had ever worked for and was delighted to see me on shift.

'Don, Kai has a doctor's appointment, nothing serious, just a quick check up. Would you like to take him? Also, it's his birthday today. He doesn't want us to celebrate or even mention it but I was thinking, after the appointment you guys can grab some lunch. He hasn't stopped complimenting you all week, he really likes you.'

My heart was thumping with excitement. I hadn't thought I would have much free time to draw out more of his story, at least not until the end of the day.

'Of course. I'd really enjoy spending the day with him.'

'Great. Instead of taking a cab, use my car – and don't scratch it,' she added with a smile.

'Really?' I was surprised; she loved her new Tesla.

'Yes, of course. It's going to be a rainy, horrible day, it won't be nice waiting for a cab. Besides, they're always late. Shame we can't get Uber in the sticks yet.'

I left the staff room and went off to start the shift feeling energised. I genuinely had a skip in my step. Our duties were to help the care users get dressed and ready for the day, take them breakfast and dispense their required medication. We had an efficient system and shared the responsibilities amongst ourselves. During my allocated obligations I had to pop up to Kai's room and remind him he had a doctor's appointment, giving him enough time to gather himself for the trip. He was happy to see me and delighted when I asked if it would be okay if I accompanied him.

'I'm ecstatic,' he declared.

A few hours later we were both in the car park, walking towards the vehicle.

'What is that?' Kai was pointing to the SUV.

'I'm not sure how to answer that question. It's different,' I replied, genuinely kerfuffled. 'It's *electric*, the new Tesla Model X.'

He looked at me and smiled, interest showing on his face. 'I've heard of them, but not yet seen one,' Kai said, genuinely amazed.

'It's an homage to the Serbian inventor and engineer, Nikola Tesla, hence the name. Many people say they care about the environment but are scared or somewhat embarrassed to be seen driving an electric vehicle, it's probably why you haven't seen many on the roads. A more sustainable form of transportation isn't quite *masculine* enough for many here in England. Hopefully, this beast will begin to convert the petrol heads.'

'It is a beast, a scintillating, beautiful beast,' Kai said as he began circling it, gently running his fingers along the immaculate, pearl-white paintwork. When I opened the passenger door for Kai, its sophisticated and minimalistic interior awed him equally as much as the seductive lines of the vehicle's body.

'I love this modern world we live in. Wish I was young again, though.' He climbed in and nestled into the seat. 'Good god, this leather is soft and pleasant.'

I smiled, closing the passenger door behind him, then nipped around to the driver's side and jumped into the plush seat, closed my door and we both simultaneously put on our seat belts.

'Safety first,' Kai said with a contented smile.

On our way to the doctor's we didn't talk about anything other than the SUV; he really was fond of it.

'So this is an all-wheel drive?'

'Yeah,' I said while concentrating on the task at hand. I'll have to work really hard after university to afford one of these, I thought to myself. It really is a great vehicle to drive and it's so worth it, being able to contribute to defending our environment from pollutants, one less or one more purchase at a time, depending on how you look at it, I guess.

I think Kai must have noticed the enjoyment etched on my face.

'I really do miss driving. Don't ever lose your mind,' he said. He sank into his seat quietly. I didn't know how to respond, but didn't have to; he asked if we could continue our journey in silence, I nodded acceptance. I did in some way understand how he must have been feeling, it was something that was always on my mind. If I ever lost control of my visions I could definitely end up "in his shoes" as the saying goes. We both remained relaxed but to a certain degree, despondent. We arrived at our destination.

The doctor was quirkily funny and cheered our spirits. The appointment was quick and pleasant and before long we were out. Kai took care of our lunch arrangements, aided by his eccentric phone. He explained it had been hand crafted here in England. 'Pure black is the colour, just like my heart,' he said with a naughty wink. I was somewhat intrigued. Actually, not really if the truth be told, but it *was* completely new to me. Then again, it would be, as I was sure it was out of my financial reach. The device appeared rather unnecessary – it had a ruby on its side emulating a button – probably created by, or for some wealthy person who had every other whimsical desire met. Presumably not having any real benefit, nor actually contributing to society, although it did appear to be able to do the same as my iPhone. Aware of my unexcited expression and clueless bewilderment, he still continued to explain how it was made, mainly from three elements: ceramic, titanium and sapphire crystal.

'What would something like that cost?' I asked dispassionately.

'Around thirteen thousand pounds, but you could pay a lot more, depending on how much you covet jewels and precious metals.'

I quietly thought to myself; yet we live in a world with so much hunger and deprivation, my mind drifting as Kai continued speaking, thinking about Jacob Riis's publication on the 1890's tenements of New York, '*How the Other Half Lives*'. Today, much has changed, but at the same time a lot hasn't. I saw Kai's wristwatch as he spoke and I thought, luckily for many, there are still some who practice philanthropy. Even large firms like his watch maker are trying to help, selling luxury to the wealthy and using much of their profits to offer compassion for our planet's sustainability. Luxury with compassion – a term I once heard used by a journalist to describe the firm's actions – at least she wasn't muckraking like some do. My cogitation ended as I tried to re-enter the conversation.

'I know it sounds rather pretentious, but these elements really do give it an extraordinary and special feel in my hands. Most importantly, it makes phone calls, which I still think is magnificent. Who knew communication on the go would become possible? This phone can do everything else as well; emails and such, apparently all done by a magical penguin but it is the 'fellow-slave' placed at my beck and call that is my favourite attribute. I can use it to easily make dining reservations with restaurants that would normally be impossible to get a table at. The service on offer, without a doubt, always finds the right people for your required job at hand. Do you want to find a gentleman's establishment? This phone can make it happen for me,' he said with a chuckle and another naughty wink.

I chuckled too. Dirty old man, I thought, and magical penguin? This description made me feel warm and fuzzy. He meant Linux's operating system and their mascot. He handed it over and asked me to use the ruby button to get us a table.

'Where? How? Wait, what?' I stood, baffled.

'Give it back.' He gestured impatiently, touched the side button and placed the phone to his ear. He must have had the volume quite high on the device because the voice of the person who came on the line was clear enough for me to hear the conversation, even though I was a few feet away.

'Good day, Mr Lele. This is Gerrard, how may I help you?' The voice was professional, efficient and warm. Kai spoke confidently as if he knew the voice.

'Hello, Gerrard. I would like a table for two at that busy Brazilian Restaurant in Plymouth.'

'Off course sir, what time would you like your reservation?'

Kai glimpsed at his steely watch, uniquely octagonal with visible screws. 'In twenty minutes.'

Momentarily a pause followed and if I had to guess, it sounded like fingers typing away on a keyboard, then

Gerrard responded, 'Your reservation is all ready for you, sir.'

'Thank you,' Kai answered, before ending the call and placing the gadget into his trouser pocket.

'Where to?' I asked, although already knowing the answer.

'A restaurant at Royal William Yard,' Kai said excitedly. 'I hope you like Brazilian.'

I knew exactly where we were heading, and the thought of it did excite my appetite. Shit, I thought, maybe I should get me a 'fellow-slave', it's impossible to get a table at that place.

Before departing I wanted to show Kai something cool, 'Wait here?' I asked him. I got into the vehicle with the driver's door still open. A few taps on the touchscreen display and the back gull-wing doors opened ceremoniously.

'Isn't that cool!' I shouted as I leant over to try to see his face as he stood, amazed.

'*It look like ah corbeaux!*' he shouted back in a broad Trini accent; it was the first time I had heard him truly sound Trinidadian. His exclamation surprised me. The vehicle was awesome but he was right, it *did* remind me of the indestructible Caribbean vulture – well, maybe if they were white. It made me laugh all the way to the restaurant.

Gloria's Bamsee

On arrival, a young waiter showed us to our table and left us with menus. Shortly after, a lovely young waitress politely introduced herself with the brightest of smiles.

'Hello, I'm Gloria. Would you like any drinks?'

'Two mojitos please,' Kai blurted out.

I smiled back at the waitress. 'Just one. I'll have a guava juice.' She nodded; I was wearing a blue tunic which most understood to be the uniform of a care assistant.

'Spoilsport,' he said while he ogled Gloria as she headed off to the bar. 'I have not seen a *Bam-se Lambe* like that in years.'

I laughed. 'I haven't heard those words in years. You're right though, it is a glorious bamsee.'

As our banter calmed he asked, 'So, where did we get to last weekend?'

I smiled and looked keenly at him. 'You had just been startled by Papa Bois and Gang Gang Sarah on a beach in

Trinidad, but can you tell me more about the little hummingbird, Silver?'

'Oh, yes, I remember now. Don't worry, we shall talk more about Silver in due course.' He continued his story right where he had left off.

'I remember you,' I said to Gang Gang Sarah, but she didn't respond.

'Thank you,' Papa Bois interrupted.

'What for?' I asked curiously.

'Giving my heart that thump. She really did kick my ass,' he joked as he swung over the bloated goatskin sack he had on his shoulder in my direction. I caught it, looking at him, confused.

'Have a drink before you pass out from dehydration,' he encouraged.

It took a little while to discover how to use it. The water tasted strange but I didn't care, I was tremendously thirsty.

I decided to tell them about the hummingbird and that it had told me to wait here beside this boat.

'We know,' they replied in chorus.

'Okay, I'll bite. How did you know?'

'It's an Amerindian longboat and we were both standing behind you and saw the whole thing,' said Sarah.

'Oh, okay. I was expecting a supernatural comeback,' I responded, frowning. 'What do we need to do now?' I asked, worried about Marita.

Again in chorus, like a double act, they both replied, 'Nothing.'

By now I had learnt the situation could easily get worse, but what was to come next I could not have envisaged. The longboat was suspended in the shallow, warm waters. From side to side it gracefully swayed like a horse during dressage. The creature's appearance was truly sudden as it leapt out of the water like an overgrown eel. Both Papa Bois and I stepped back. Sarah did not budge.

'Mama De L'eau,' she whispered under her breath. Sarah looked at me, strange and cold. 'Malliouhanna is what she calls herself when she transforms into a human woman. When she's in *this* form we call her Mama De L'eau. Her conviction is always uncertain, but regrettably, we need her.'

If fear had a colour, it would have been the pale complexion my face emitted in that restaurant, as I was sure Kai was talking about the same woman whom I had met so strangely on the train in New York and who had vanished on the beach in Exmouth. I didn't distract Kai and he continued.

The living thing was unique, similar to a mermaid; part woman with the lower half more like the anatomy of a large snake or eel. Her lower body coiled around the longboat, taking charge of the still-floating vessel. Her bare upper body curled up on the prow, becoming one with the vessel as she held on to it. Now looking like a living figurehead, she spoke. '*Board, we late.*'

Sarah did not hesitate, she waded into the water and climbed aboard. I followed. Papa Bois did as well but he was clearly hesitant. Seating was available between her coils but the planks were slippery. Slime dripped from her incongruous frame, it was warm and smelt of cod liver oil. She seemed eager to please but not in an unctuous way. Who was she sent by? Was it Silver? And was Silver sent by someone else? I was questioning everything. Nevertheless, we were on our way.

'We'll be in Barbados before nightfall,' Sarah said. Papa Bois and I remained silent. Mama De L'eau said nothing. Her magical frame pulled the longboat like a sledge, skimming the water at high speeds.

The freedom of being out in the elements, from serene sunshine to perilous thunderstorms, has never eluded me. I have always loved sailing across the sea even when it was difficult, stopping at different islands to fill up on provisions, mainly rum, and the opportunity of exploring new women as I had done on many of my previous voyages across the Pacific: "The Peaceful Sea", as Ferdinand Magellan named it in 1521. But this was different. I began feeling like a pirate, filled with rage, like an irked ghost passing through. Some time later, leaning on Papa Bois, I fell asleep.

I jumped awake. Impossible I thought, who could sleep through this? I must have been truly enervated from the day's events. Papa Bois, declaring his dislike of the ocean, looked as though he were about to be sick. Sarah snapped her fingers and a wooden bucket appeared between his legs.

'It's one thing sitting in slime, but sitting in vomit—' she said, still with her cold demeanour.

'I hate boats,' he scowled, jerking back and forth, head bent over, trying to stay positioned atop the bucket. I pitied him. Who is he? I thought to myself before enquiring of Sarah, with a sullen look and a touch of curiosity.

Her expression remained deadpan as she responded. 'He's the father of the forests and all they surround, protector of the trees, birds, animals and the bees.' She was now looking directly at me with fury in her eyes; anger in her voice followed. 'Poachers, hunters, and anyone causing danger to the wildlife or the forest should fear him, especially when his devilish horns are on display.'

Her grim tone reminded me, as I had slept, a memory had returned as a dream. I single-handedly sailed the Pacific many times but only once was I ever in serious trouble. It was night and I was almost at my mysterious destination, the island of Luna Puesta; roughly translated, 'Moon that has set'. The island was discovered by a Portuguese sailor, Pedro Fernández de Quirós, in 1606. I have always been fascinated by sharks and this unique island was home to many species. Truth be told, I don't know what persuaded me to embark on that particular solo journey; what I do know is that I experienced severe titillation from it. Something smashed into my yacht, the timber frame snapped like a twig, leaving me in the deadly waters, drifting on wreckage, during the night. Something continued to circle me. I saw the creature, I know I did, the same creature that had devastated my keel. It was ill-lit but the entity seemed to be a shimmery green with a long reptilian body, large scales and a huge fan on its back. Even to this day, I swear it was a dragon and I felt as though it wanted to vanquish me. I was rescued before the creature could finish me off, picked up by a Filipino freight ship. How they saw me, I do not know. I had never known fear until that night. I was paralysed with it, clutching onto the debris; my rescuers said I must have survived through strength and sheer will. Some strange coercion had taken command of my body and tightened my grip of that wreckage, or it was plain luck.

I was a different person then. Now, completely in love, Marita brought out the best in me. I had to save her. I needed to muster up that same strength and will, even though I knew it may cost me my life. Given the opportunity, I would sacrifice myself for my betrothed without hesitation.

The weather had seemed unresolved before we left but the brewing storm was now upon us. The ether lashed at us with anger: lightning sliced through the celestial vastness; thunder roared like an injured, angry lion. We were drenched from both the sea spray and the turbulent rain. Papa Bois was overwhelmed and vomiting—not always in the bucket. The large half-sea serpent hurtling our boat towards Barbados was certainly not our only fear; it indubitably felt as though the weather was trying to stop us.

'Crane beach!' Sarah shouted and pointed.

Kai stopped talking as Gloria approached our table with the drinks and to take our order. We were ready, and he chose the pollo foresta: a chicken breast sliced and smothered in a creamy smoked chipotle mushroom sauce, served with spring onion rice and fine green beans. I ordered the seafood moqueca: a mild tomato and coconut curry of sustainable white fish, prawns, chunky squash, palm hearts, spinach, peppers, fresh tomatoes and sweet chunky plantain, all piled on spring onion rice with coconut farofa to sprinkle. We asked for more drinks and after taking our order Gloria left our table, and as before, we both stared at her bamsee. I felt a little guilty for doing so but it really was splendid.

Kai took a drink of his mojito and continued. He had my complete attention.

'Get the longboat off the beach and I will return for you all at day break!' Mama De L'eau wailed out against the resonance of the wind and sea, before throwing herself into the dark Caribbean waters.

Arriving at the beach in this supernatural whirlwind was undoubtedly a miracle. We were frazzled like a *chikee-chong* battered in the storm, but still disembarked like ferocious eighth century Northmen. The night was humid, the storm persistent and strangely, the tide was not in. We pulled our longboat closer to the shore in the gale-force winds, drenched by relentless missiles in the form of heavy raindrops. Because of my recent experiences on these Caribbean beaches, I was alert. After securing the longboat Gang Gang Sarah pointed to an indistinct fire in the distance. Head down I followed her in the direction of the flame. I felt somewhat safe with her, although not entirely sure why.

I had never been to Crane Beach, I thought as I looked at my watch. It was not working, the dials kept spinning round and round. 'Impossible!' I exclaimed, annoyed. 'It's a Royal Oak, this watch will never stop working.'

'It's not your fancy watch,' Sarah called out as she continued up the beach. 'It's just this place, time has no power here.'

Papa Bois came up behind me and patted my shoulder.

'It's not even three p.m.,' he bellowed, looking up at the lightning-infested sky. 'Don't worry, we'll get her back.' He signalled me to pull back, away from Sarah. When he felt she was out of earshot with her back to us, he pounced on me.

'Caution is required with her, nothing is what it seems,' he said, looking towards her, then looking back at me he added, 'Annie is not a witch, not even a woman but instead, a great *Apu* or mountain spirit. This supreme being can live in both the middle and upper worlds and can intercede for humanity, do not fear it.' He raised his finger to his lips, gesturing to be quiet as we caught up with Sarah.

'You two head over to the fire. I'll be back,' Papa Bois said as he marched off, his hooves digging into the sand as we watched him disappear into the saturated darkness, away from the flickering light.

Sarah did not say anything. Instead, she continued her route and I followed. We got there to discover the fire burning in a pit within a coastal cove. Two coconut tree stumps lay either side of the fire, to be used as benches, it appeared. 'He has been expecting us,' she said, pointing at a cauldron covered by singed banana leaves. It was above a smaller radiant flame, hovering, aided by three rocks making a tripod-like cooking device with the burning coals in the middle. The smells coming from the contrivance were very pleasing. The cove offered shelter and privacy for what we needed to do.

'Sit, get a calabash *bolee* and eat something.' She calmly pushed me towards the cauldron as she spoke. There were carved wooden spoons among the makeshift utensils, they were interestingly enchanting and I was hungry, but I could not eat.

Sarah began getting undressed. I was perplexed, her body beautifully shaped, but her back was covered in a mixture of scars. It looked as though she had been flogged on numerous occasions. The contusions were raised, bloody and appeared raw. She wore a heavy, hooded, silk cotton robe and had been completely covered except for her face throughout the course of our journey. Placing her wet robe on one of the stumps to dry, she sat on the other stump in front the fire. She was completely naked, but instead of an old hunched woman, she was now much younger, sylph-like and beautiful. Her body language did not make me feel uncomfortable, instead what she did made sense to me. I did the same and after getting undressed I sat next to her. It was much warmer.

'Can I see to your back?' I asked, concerned. 'It looks sore.'

'No.' She was abrupt, but then apologetic. 'Sorry,' she said. 'It's okay, there's nothing you can do.'

'Were you whipped?'

'Yes, and even though it was a long time ago it will never heal, the whip used was an evil thing.'

'When did this happen?' I sympathetically demanded. 'How can a human being do something so horrific to another?'

'Humans have always been dreadful creatures. The year was 1833, a hundred and forty-four years ago. I remember it well, but enough about the past, we are here to ensure a future.' Her head lowered as she spoke.

Not wanting to upset her even more and not realising how old she actually was, I stopped talking. My thoughts turned to Marita. I missed her, I was worried about her and my forthcoming child. Although hostages, I hoped they were being treated reasonably well.

Some time later, still seated in front of the fire, now propped up leaning on each other, we were dozing, worn out after that testing trip.

Mr Bones

I was awoken suddenly by a gruff male voice. 'Your clothes are dry now.' The voice echoed, but no one was in sight.

'Did you hear that? Was it Papa Bois? He must have returned,' I said as I jumped awake, wincing as I got a splinter in my ass cheek during the process.

'Yes I did, but it wasn't Papa Bois.' Although standing, she did not seem startled. As we got dressed a man with an unusually small head appeared to be walking out of the cavernous cove wall. There was no doorway, just the jagged stone. Was it a gateway? I thought. Gang Gang Sarah looked pleased to see him. They greeted each other and then she introduced us.

'Mr Bones, this is Kai. Kai, this is Mr Bones.' Strangely, and maybe I did not notice initially when he appeared but for the first time, Sarah seemed nervous. He went over to the food and began helping himself.

'Do you trust that I'm good?' Sarah asked me.

Remembering the warning from Papa Bois, I lied.

'Yes, I believe so. I cannot say I do completely but your aura seems good. Ms Hilda saved my life once and now you are here, saying she sent you.' I needed her help and had to sound convincing. I thought about it a bit more. 'Yes, I do trust you,' I declared more confidently.

'Good. Mr Bones is an ancient and powerful immortal Vodou priest. He can help us find Marita but you have to do everything he asks of you.'

'I will.' My response came without hesitation. It was the truth, I would do anything to retrieve Marita.

While talking I had been attentive to what Mr Bones was doing. He took the makeshift lid off the cauldron and to my bewilderment it was empty, but he picked up a bolee and spoon anyway. He dipped the bolee into the empty pot and retrieved it, full of food.

'How did you do that?' I asked.

'Whatever you feel like eating will appear in the bolee. These folkloric bolees were made by an old thaumaturgist from a legendary calabash tree which only grows on Lanse Aux Epines beach in Grenada. My favourite meal is this Bajan national dish, coucou and flying fish,' he described, as his meal attempted to fly from his bolee. He settled on one of the coconut stumps to eat.

The sustenance, although off-putting, but interesting, was overshadowed but the irresistible aromas. I needed no more encouragement. When I retrieved my bolee from the bottom of the deep pot it was filled with oil down, Grenada's national dish. I remembered Maria would make this meal when I was a boy, I loved it. I sat on the opposite stump with Sarah, a grin on my face like a Cheshire cat.

'Ahh, good choice,' Mr Bones said.

Sarah looked at me a little more seriously and spoke to me as though he were not present.

'Mr Bones was placed on earth to do the biddings of Shangor.'

'What or who is Shangor?' I asked, once again bewildered; so much I did not understand.

'Shangor is one of the main deities of the African religious beliefs of Shango. He is the possessor of fire, lightning, thunder and the bringer of war but he is also the instigator of drumming, dancing and frolicking.' Her words triggered a memory of when I was a boy living in Fyzabad and I had been to a religious ceremony at a friend's house. Their religious beliefs were different but this was normal and we all respected each other nonetheless. The lady hosting this ceremony was a Shango Baptist; my father had once explained to me that this was a fusion of both Christianity and African beliefs. They would conduct these atypical ceremonies every few years, but then again, which religion has a *typical* ceremony? The service was grand, their families and friends would visit from all over the world to be present. I only ever attended once. Together they would sacrifice animals and make offerings of the animal's blood, together with a variety of other items into an *open house*: a small enclosure, almost like an animal pen with bamboo poles, sprouting out of the ground, high into the air, flying flags. Each pole flew a different coloured banner representing an individual Shango spirit. The offerings were placed at the base of each flagpole. I remembered the black flag; it belonged to Mr Bones. He was the spirit which demanded the blood sacrifice.

I looked at Mr Bones again. Although sitting, I could still see he had an extremely tall and gaunt frame, centuries of wisdom etched on his face. His demeanour seemed calm but calculating, accompanied by the blackest of eyes; they were large and sunken. He seemed relaxed but still there was a hard stare each time he looked at me, almost as if he was trying to read my thoughts. He wore old dingy khaki trousers, his upper body topless with unnatural stripes on his shoulders and face – like a tiger or other predator – and a pair of over-worn leather sandals partly clad his dirty, ashy feet. He wore an old leather satchel across his body and an amulet hung from his neck, it looked like a miniature animal head and more bones hung from his ears and hair.

'Do not call me Bones, it is normally used to project fear. You have nothing to fear from me. Instead, call me Siba.' His voice was phantasmal and intimidating, perfect for conjuring, I supposed. No matter what he said to convince me, I knew I was out of my depth. While on the longboat, Sarah had said he was the best conjurer of spells she knew and that he would help us to find the La Diablesse or maybe even show what would come to pass. Revealing our future and giving us a better understanding of our predicament would unequivocally put us at an advantage, but at a cost, she reckoned. I told her I did not care about the cost, I was willing to bear it no matter what. I had to try anything to win my family back; not just Marita and Nancy, but everyone else who had been on that yacht. I had to try.

Siba's hard stare transformed into a grin, I thought it was because of the bewildered look still on my face, from him walking through a wall or the bolee trick. I probably should not have been surprised after the things that I had witnessed over the past couple of days.

'You would not believe, I have existed for many millennia and still I am excitable. I really am happy to finally meet you. I knew this day was coming since the last time I saw your mother and you really do look just like her.' He spoke very quickly while still eating as though the food was scalding his mouth.

'What do you mean?' I blurted out.

'You're the spitting image of her,' he partially chuckled, while still chewing and shaking his head in what appeared to be a joyful mannerism.

Everyone had always told me that I looked like my father; this was a first. I sat speechless, questions rushing through my mind but I could not find the words to murmur a single sound, utter silence. Frozen in disbelief.

He cut the silence.

'Future knowledge of this world and the next is possible, but the price to pay is precisely one pound of flesh from my own body, hence I do not normally perform this service. In fact, the only other persons I have ever performed this sacrifice for was you and your mother. You were already inside her. She knew this day would come and had been looking for a way to protect you from it. What Madinina and I didn't know was that she would die giving birth to you the very next day. You, her unborn child, was all she cared about.'

'You were supposed to be her new beginning, but instead, you were her demise,' Sarah said, as she joined the conversation. Siba shot her an ominous look before turning back to me.

'She was certain about her decision to have you even though she knew what could come next, but you really did mean the world to her. My only regret is she never got the opportunity to hold you before her last breath, she was gone before you left her womb. Those quacks had to cut you out. She was my daughter, I knew her heart and felt her pain. You might not believe me but I genuinely care about you as well, you are very dear to me. Sarah doesn't agree with me. I'm not meant to intervene but I had to, you are all I have left.'

If I thought I was shocked before by all this strangeness, Siba's revelations sent me into an inner panic.

Some time between finishing eating and standing, his spoon had transformed into an old rusty knife. Handing his empty bolee to Sarah, he pulled on the skin from one side of his stomach and without notice he began cutting. There was no blood, just dust. He then placed the dry piece of flesh within the bolee.

'There, precisely one pound.'

I had not touched my food and now for certain there was no way I could eat.

'I had two daughters, your mother and Ayiti. You've met Ayiti already—she took Marita. I never thought I would lose them, they had everlasting life just like myself. Ayiti was the eldest. She was blighted by an evil witch of a woman who summoned the darkest of spell-working that should never be used. The sinful hex removed the soul from my daughter's undying body. Madinina, your mother, forced me to revoke her everlastingness because she was in love with your father, a mortal. She desired mortality and a normal life with a family. I granted her request only because I saw how truly happy she was, for the first time in nearly four hundred years. When Madinina fell pregnant with you she knew something was wrong. She suspected her baby was in danger, as though a dark force was coming for you. She came to me to protect you, we wanted to keep you safe so I granted you immortality. I did not possess the strength to restore Madinina's immortality at the same time, she was supposed to return when I had recovered. The very next day she went into labour before I could—' he paused, his voice now cracking. 'I had Gang Gang Sarah find you.'

Sarah intervened, 'Until yesterday we all thought Ayiti had been forever lost. Her body has been hidden from us for the past hundred and forty-four years. Since it happened we haven't stopped looking for her, despite not gathering a single clue.'

Siba, now more collected, continued. 'Until now. The woman who violated Ayiti and disrespected her corpse was a plantation owner in Jamaica. Her name was Annie Palmer or rather, that was the alias she used. She was dubbed the White Witch of Rose Hall. Annie was the mistress of the sugar cane plantation. It was alleged that she murdered her way to her fortune, each time viciously killing her husbands then having them buried under individual palm trees on the coastal borders of the estate. These were all rumours. However, what was certain was that she married three times. The stories were passed down over the years – the memories of Annie's ferocious appetite for inflicting pain and suffering. It was unquenchable and created a combination of control, hatred and fear over her slaves and her so-called equals. Many tales grew while she reigned at Rose Hall from 1818 right through to her demise in 1833, some true, some fictitious.

'The Rose Hall great house had a balcony built on the second floor to the back of the mansion, overlooking the whipping post in the grounds. The vantage point was perfect for Annie to enjoy the onslaught of blows at her command while she took delight from the shade in the Caribbean heat. Her *whopping boy* wore a grim mask at all times. There was no reason to hide his face, maybe he was disfigured, or it was for intimidation purposes, who knows? Annie had a special whip made for him from a dried bull's penis, tipped with three threads ending with small metal balls like a hydra which he called his *Bull-Pistle*. A single stroke was enough to remove flesh and incapacitate the victim with pain. Sarah knows of this first hand.'

That is what happened to Sarah's back, I thought, but I did not interrupt and Siba continued explaining Annie's origins.

Gloria and the waiter who seated us earlier returned with our food. It looked great. This time, we were so distracted by our plates, neither of us gave Gloria's bamsee another thought or look. Like true Trinidadians the only distraction from a beautiful woman was good food. We devoured our meal, partaking in nothing more than idle and playful chit-chat. It was then that Kai asked a favour of me.

'Have you ever been to Jay's Grave?'

'Sort of, have you?'

He shook his head, his response sorrowful. 'Can you take me to see it?' he asked.

'We have time before we're expected home and it's only a thirty-minute drive. Of course we can go,' I replied with an encouraging smile.

He smiled in return, but not like he normally would. He seemed different and then proceeded to describe the mystery of the grave. He explained how the remains lay in a small mound at the side of a crossroads in the green lanes leading to Dartmoor National Park. Unfortunately there were probably no obsequies kept for her. Not much was known about her by the locals, and all was based on speculation and local legend which dictated she was an eighteenth-century suicide case. Back then, victims of suicide would be given no Christian rites and instead were buried at a crossroads, staked to the ground to prevent them rising from their shallow graves.

'This religious stupidity infuriates me,' Kai protested. 'I hope a day will come when we will stop being indoctrinated by fictional characters and truly treat our fellow man with the love and respect we all so deeply desire in both life and death.'

Although the mood was now somewhat morbid, we enjoyed our meal. Skipping desert seemed fitting to the conversation; we paid and left. I knew where the grave was, as part of the University Bike Club we cycled past it on numerous occasions. I had never stopped, but thought the site looked lonely but beautiful. It was a pretty drive, but Kai still remained a bit gloomy, or maybe it was the large meal he had just conquered. I was unsure.

It was not long before we arrived. Surprisingly, Kai asked me to stay in the vehicle. He behaved as though the lost, tormented body trapped there meant something to him. I sat and watched him walk over to the curious grave. The black cape-like coat he wore had a hood which he pulled over his head to shelter from the drizzling English rain. Although having spent time with this cloaked figure I was still unsure who he really was, he truly fascinated me. While he stood there I was certain I saw a green shrub grow with delicate white flowers, it looked like Lady of the Night. I was quite confident it was not there before. I remembered as a child in Trinidad, when that flower was smelt at night many believed all sorts of ghosts and unbenevolent creatures were not far behind. The realisation instantaneously presented itself. That must be the resting place of Marita.

A short while later he got back into the vehicle. 'Heated seats, I still cannot get my head around that.' His voice sounded shaken. 'Would you like me to tell you more?' he asked.

Hesitantly I replied. 'Please, go on.'

Siba explained that Gang Gang Sarah was an African witch. She had come to the Caribbean in 1818 accidentally. The villagers, back in her small African village, kidnapped and sold her younger sister into slavery but before setting off in search of her sister, Sarah, equipped with supernatural powers, cursed the village and shortly after, the entire population were enslaved. With the ability of flight, Sarah flew day and night in search of her sister, only never to prevail. Many years had now passed and Sarah became a wanderer, not wanting to return to Africa without her sister. One night, while in mid flight, she was violently blown off course by gale force winds and hurled towards the island of Tobago, landing in the village of Les Coteaux. It was a new land she had not yet been to. The search for her sister continued but no discoveries were made. While on this lush island, probing the Golden Lane Plantation, she met a slave boy she had grown up with back in Africa; his name was Tom. Sarah and Tom fell hopelessly in love, but Sarah would not stay. Their chance encounter fuelled her drive to continue looking further, she just could not give up on the search for her sister. Tom knew this. He also knew Sarah was a witch with supernatural powers, a good woman but a witch nonetheless. Because of the selfishness of most men and even with Tom's understanding of the bond and love Sarah shared with her sister, he tricked her into staying with him. One night while Sarah was visiting Tom at the sugar plantation, he made her dinner – salt-fish and steamed bananas – but there was something sinister here at work. Tom placed three nuggets of a special rock salt in the salt-fish, it was a potion he purchased with his soul to take away the powers of Gang Gang Sarah. Unaware of Tom's treachery and the loss of her powers, Sarah took off into flight and later that night, her powers dissolved. She fell from the skies into the branches of a tree, preventing her certain death but she was still gravely injured. Tom foolishly thought, once unable to continue her quest, Sarah would return to him. This never happened.

'Ayiti found her and brought her to me,' Siba continued. 'They were close right until Annie destroyed Ayiti. When Sarah tried to retrieve Ayiti's body, Annie had her caught and punished severely. Shango only permits me to practice white magic, black obeah is absolutely forbidden, except for one dark curse allowed only if someone really deserves it, and Annie deserved all the cruelty both man and gods could muster upon her. She was as stubborn as she was evil and vowed she would never say where Ayiti's body was hidden.

'The one dark spell I possessed was sufficient and more powerful than her black talents, and I used it willingly. Knowing she was the only person with the knowledge of Ayiti's location I could not kill her, even though I wanted to, more than you can ever comprehend. Instead, I took away her black gifts before banishing her soul into the abyss, just as she had done to my sweet Ayiti. I then had the white witch's body placed in a tomb on her own grounds, a tomb that will keep her there securely, locked away for all of time.' He sighed, his dark eyes looking at me directly. 'Nothing is as it seems, the world is filled with many mysteries and mismatched forces. Unfortunately, I cannot share them all with you, for lack of time.'

'Could we begin?' I asked.

Siba hesitated. With his intimidating gaze he bored into me up and down, before nodding his head in acceptance. With a fresh smile on his face, he opened a bottle of the same Black Barrel rum which he pulled from his satchel. He poured the golden potion onto the ground, creating a large circumference around ourselves and the fire. 'It's for our protection,' he said as he continued to pour until the bottle was empty. He corked the bottle and placed it back in the satchel. On removing his hand, he retrieved several bouquets of herbs. Stretching his long limbs, he hung the herbs on metal pins in the stone ceiling, once used for hanging shackles.

'Is that for our protection as well?' I asked.

'Yes. A quick learner, just like your mother,' he responded lightheartedly.

He retrieved the rum bottle from his satchel once more and handed it to me. I accepted it, expecting it to be empty but there was something in it, a small black figure.

'What is it?' I asked lifting the bottle, intently trying to decipher what was inside.

'It's a *Baccoo*, don't forget to feed him. He likes fresh breast milk.'

It was a tiny, pitch black, bearded man, with the whitest of eyes, caught inside the bottle.

'You mean from a woman? Where the hell am I supposed to find fresh breast milk? What do I do with it?' I asked, still squinting into the bottle.

'He can tell you of the future and give you immense wealth,' Siba replied.

I was already wealthy, but a fortune teller on demand? This could be interesting. As I stood, baffled, Sarah brushed past me muttering, 'At least he didn't give you the Heartman.'

'What?'

Bones pulled out a strange mask from his satchel, leaning into it as he placed it over his face. It had a striking likeness to something or someone familiar, but then all skulls look similar. It was a perfect fit and actually made him look whole, as if that was the reason for his irregularly small head – to be able to wear someone else's skeleton. Siba now stood in front of me with two calabash bolees, one filled with some kind of liquid, the other with a powdery substance.

'Get undressed,' he said.

I did so after cautiously placing the little man trapped in the rum bottle on the ground. He lifted the bolee with the powdery substance.

'Crushed seeds from the Anadenanthera peregrina tree.' He then lifted the other bolee, passing it to me.

'Drink all,' he said. I accepted it, staring at the murky liquid before downing it all.

'Yuk.' It was bitter. 'What was it?'

Before Siba could answer I emitted a tremendous fart with the most repulsive of smells and sick began spewing out of my mouth with great force. Without warning, faeces followed from my rear.

'You cannot enter the dream world without being completely purged of *this* world. Senna and Epsom salts always does the trick,' Siba said, 'with an additional something extra for haste.' With these words he dashed the bolee of powder into my face. Naked and covered in this concoction, I fell back into my excrement and other bodily fluids. While falling I heard his voice becoming fainter.

'Cohoba will get you there,' he said.

It felt as though I was falling for a long, long, long time and all around me was confusingly kaleidoscopic. I must have blacked out.

Epilogue

'*Deep into that darkness peering, long I stood there, wondering, fearing, doubting, dreaming dreams no mortal ever dared to dream before.*'

Edgar Allan Poe

Trèz

I awoke later in a cold sweat, lying flat on my back, unsure as to how long I had been unconscious. The ground beneath me felt cold and sticky on my bare body. I lay there, in and out of consciousness. It was so bright, every time I re-opened my eyes they felt sore; it took a while before they adjusted. My voice anxious, I began calling out for Sarah and Siba, my shouts becoming louder, a more fearful tone occupying my voice. They were not visible, but *nothing* was, except for a thick dark fog, or was it smoke? I was uncertain. 'Maybe it's concussion,' I said out loud to myself while sniffing the air like a bloodhound.

Kai leant over slightly in the plush upholstery of the SUV, looking even deeper than he normally does, into my eyes.

'Black fire is what came to mind while sniffing.' He paused. 'I was a volunteer firefighter a long time ago, before all this happened. I know fires.' He sat back slowly, adjusting his seatbelt as he continued to explain. 'Black fire is a phrase used to aptly describe a type of black smoke that is high-volume, turbulent velocity and ultra-dense, but I had never seen smoke like this before. It was not consistently black, but a mixture of greys and whites, aggressively swirling within a violent wind. This made no sense. The temperature was uncomfortably high. I knew black fire could reach temperatures of more than a thousand degrees Fahrenheit and we were trained to treat it as actual flames. It was equally dangerous, if not worse, yet I was breathing fine. If it was smoke, I would have been struggling to breathe and strangely, it was not as bright as I had thought it was initially. I reluctantly rolled over. It was painful; my entire body ached, especially the back of my head. I slowly climbed onto my knees with my elbows and palms on the ground, stretching an arch in my back like a scared cat. Where am I? I thought, perplexed, as I tried to climb up off the floor, and why is the ground sticky? Slowly I lifted my right palm. In these hard-to-see conditions it seemed to be blood, was it mine? As the thought sank in I touched the back of my head. My hair was soggy. I placed my hand close to my face for clarity. More blood. My hands were now covered in it; my own blood, it seemed. The back of my head had burst open, the blood had begun coagulating. I must have been lying there for some time.

I looked around as I struggled to stand. All I could see was the dirty smog, even on the ground. I was standing in it and reluctant to take a step in case I plummeted again, this time to my certain doom as I feared I could not cope with my fragile body crashing to the floor once more. As I tried to see through the fog, I felt relief as I realised Silver, the white hummingbird, was hovering in front of me, her tiny wings manoeuvring her levitation.

'Always appear to help me find my way,' I uttered with a mixture of confidence and exasperation, finishing with a sigh of relief.

'How was your journey? asked the tiny voice.

I reached out to touch her but she vanished, just as she had before, into a puff of delicate smoke. I felt nauseous, she could not leave me here. Her silvery mist hung in the air, not dissipating as it should with the violent wind; everything had stopped. A smoggy stillness began thickening as though it were alive; the smoke began to swirl independently and captivatingly, it held my full attention. A woman began to appear. She was undraped, the swirling clouds her gown. I could see her athletically-toned physique, almost masculine but she was unmistakably a woman. Her upper body now completely visible, free of her mystical gown. She was looking directly at me.

'Annie?' I asked reposefully, so as not to cause alarm. Her hair was wet, flowing down her neck either side of her shoulders, running over her collarbones. The tilt of her head and confident smirk in itself left me uneasy. Her voice, soft and tantalising, acknowledged me.

'Sort of. I have been known by many names and yes, I reckon I was once called that. You were thinking about me. Don't be timid, I can feel your desire, that's why I am here.'

An eternal few seconds followed. Again she spoke, exuding serene confidence. 'I have always been with you, although at first I did not have to worry much because your watcher, Ms Hilda, was there, but when you lost her—when *we* lost her, I had to come myself. Silver seemed a safe disguise.'

My expression was a giveaway of my confusion condensing, all coming together with this new-found coherence. 'If Ms Hilda was protecting me for you—Ayiti *allowed* the douens to pummel me? So where do Siba and Sarah come into the scenario?'

'Not just a pretty face, I see,' she hissed. 'I think they were only meant to domineer you. The prophecy said only her own blood could free her, I don't expect she wanted you extinguished. Siba and Sarah—' she said, snickering, with an almost amorous inclination.

'What prophecy?' Why did Siba and Sarah not tell me of this? I thought.

She did not respond. The intensity of her curiosity growing, she was now so close to me I could smell her. My sense of smell felt more powerful and in actuality, I relished her aroma. Slowly and seductively she began circling me, her lower body still engulfed in smoke, her right hand willingly wandering, gently stroking my physique intermittently. As she spoke, goosebumps arose on my body, not entirely from fear.

Everything I had been told about her had created an internal bias but still, this was not what I was expecting. I had anticipated a sort of cruel ghost, I guess, but here she was, in the flesh, touching me, intimidating me, arousing me. She knew that with all her appeal, she was still menacing and as though she could read my mind she whispered, 'I'm scaring you, but you're enjoying it, I know.'

She was right. Before Marita, I was encompassed by beautiful women. I would feel great delectation from them all trying to lead me astray, or even in the direction of marriage. She smiled because I did not deny it. Besides, I felt as though I had known her my entire life. I dare not reveal it to her, but my confidence, she had.

'Intimidation, fear, seduction, all can be used as tools for enjoyment if we would only allow it,' she persisted. 'Seduction begins unknowingly. Both bodies secrete pheromones, enticing a hint of excitement. The allure grows with small glances, gestures, magnetism through gentle strokes and soft consensual kisses, then we start losing self-control to an insatiable hunger for one another.' I was dizzy. She kept circling me. My roaming eyes following her round and round, but I was also completely consumed by her intoxicating beauty and charm.

'I desire seduction,' she continued. 'In fact, I fantasise about it, my prurient curiosity feeding my many different fantasies. The truth is, we all *love* being seduced and used for pleasure, but for women this is provided it is on their own terms. It is false and completely irrational for any man to believe it is okay to dominate women solely for his own pleasure.' I could feel her lips close to my ear, her icy cold whisper suggestive. 'Or is it?' She quickly pulled away and continued circling me once more. 'While some women may enjoy being dominated, unless consensual, it is a big no-no. Like *all* women, only when I feel safe and comfortable can that rush of excitement devour my body. To be dominated by you, if that is what you want—' She winked. I was speechless, shivering, I think.

'Until that feeling arises I take great pleasure in assuming the role of your temptress, teasing you, making you quiver at my every whisper.' Her stare now challenging mine as she playfully snapped her teeth. 'Allow me to take charge. It doesn't make you less of a man, but rather you become a more pleasurable one.'

She circled once more, stopping directly in front of me. The fog seemed to lift her closer, her piercing eyes holding me, her lips so close, almost touching mine. I could feel her lustful breath on my face, now purposefully warm. She whispered enticingly, 'And you may live, for ever and ever, with me.'

The gleam in her eyes clouded, her tone toughened and her demeanour became rigid as she continued to circle. 'My world thinks I'm a monster. Actually, yes, I am, in the true sense of the word and all I ever wanted was to be pleasured, and adored of course, while in my human form. Not necessarily on my own terms, just fairly.' Her glance trapped mine once more, the cloud in her inky eyes lifted.

'Do you think you can be fair with me?' she goaded mischievously.

I responded confidently. 'I can, but would it be reciprocated without discrimination?'

'Of course it will,' she sharply snapped back.

'Good, let's see then,' my tone more stern and braver now. 'Where is Ayiti's body hidden?'

She held a long pause. *Snap, snap*, she snapped her teeth at me more aggressively, but then partially smiled. 'The dead are closer to us than the living. The living will always be so very distant, caught up in their own lost lives,' she whispered, just before seductively biting my chapped lips. Her breath was icy, once more her demeanour menacing, but I did not stop her, or even dare to try. She looked down towards my exposed body; she giggled as she confidently glided back just a few feet away from me, playfully spinning, her arms gracefully swirling her smoky robes. She toyed with me, her mystical gown vanishing as the fog dissipated, leaving her completely naked, as I was. Her expression was triumphantly assured.

'There, now we are equals.'

I stuttered, unable to respond or at least a response that made sense. Without moving, she spoke firmly but still with a seductive tone.

'Humans understand nothing. Desire will be your certain destruction.'

'Where is Ayiti's body?' I stupidly and impatiently demanded.

'It doesn't work like that. Make me believe once more and I will tell.' Her smile had turned sinister.

'How? And believe in what? I can't even offer freedom. Siba told me it was impossible to get you out of here!'

Again she sniggered, this time like someone who knew all.

'That old fool thinks his dark incantations are the most powerful in these lands, he does not understand the true essence of power. *Truth*, that is where the real power lies. You humans always believe in something of nonsense, anything other than yourselves, always, why? I don't understand,' shaking her head disapprovingly.

The turn of her tempestuous mood drew the fog back in violently. I could no longer see her but could hear her voice still in front of me, towering above as though she had grown. It was eerie, ghostlike, godlike. Her tone hardened.

'Ayiti is the La Diablesse as you already know, translated from French Creole. She is a devilish temptress who has been through the gates of hell and has given him – the devil, for want of a better word – control over her soul. Whether she has relinquished her soul for gain is unknown, the only certainty is that she is directly entwined like mating snakes with the cacodemon. While her enthralling bewitchment and curvaceous figure are adequate to coax nigh on any man, she is never what she seems. Her eyes red as the glow of burning coals, her heart gloomy as night, a face partially decomposed like the grim discovery of a corpse weeks after death, all hidden, sometimes by an elaborate veil and sometimes with a wide-brimmed hat.

'She roams the night, always meticulously dressed in a beautiful silk, leg of goat blouse. To complete her outfit, her slender legs are adorned in a long petticoated skirt, one exquisite leg and boot on display via a slit, with the aim to distract her admirers from the other, covered in hair like a beast, with a cloven hoof attached. This is her true identity. Even if you manage to unite her now more tainted soul with her hollow corpse, she will never change. This is who she is and will always be.

'Ayiti is famed for utilising her mystique and power of persuasion over men and lures them into the forest to their everlasting doom. Through her spell of seduction she leads them deep into the night, knowing when they are completely unable to find their way back, then like a phantom in the darkness, she vanishes. Powerless in their lost state, her victims all share a similar fate, either staggering around to their demise, plummeting to their deaths or being viciously set upon by wild animals. Many deserve her cruelty and now I believe humanity should be punished for its brutality. As for the douens, they do her every bidding. Without a doubt, they are under her disturbed motherly yoke.

'Do not for a second believe religion will protect you all from such wickedness. It is fickle, like most humans. On many occasions and for as long as they have roamed the earth, mankind has used misguided beliefs as their excuse to domineer their surroundings.'

The fog remained dense. She sighed, her breath brushing the back of my neck. 'Marita is a prisoner in Trinidad.'

I spun around, still unable to see her.

'When under Spanish rule the island was dominated by Catholicism, then strengthened by the French during the Haitian revolutions. I was there,' she stated. 'The British brought Anglicanism while Protestantism tagged along. The act of slavery forcibly transferred the Shango, or Orisha faith, an ideology believed to have been derived from Africa as amalgamations of Protestant-African churches, then indentured workers transported with them Hinduism and Moslem beliefs. Now, modern fundamentalism brings with it Evangelical or Pentecostal churches. Only a small portion of the Caribbean islands are inhabited, yet within this small ecosystem there are many different religions.

'Bones believes I am a prisoner in this burial chamber here in Jamaica. I choose to remain here. This world is choked by unnecessary suffering and destruction. Why would I want to emerge, other than to punish society's misconduct?' Her voice echoing in a vortex all around me, she laughed sarcastically as she continued.

'Jamaica's constitution protects freedom of worship, yet most of the island's inhabitants are Protestants. Notably, a large number of religious followers classify themselves to mixed denominations using the name Church of God. Which god? I am confused about that. The smallest fraction belongs to the Roman Catholic and Anglican churches, which is interesting in itself as Anglicanism held the island's only established church right up until 1870. Here the Jewish community is one of the oldest in the Western Hemisphere, there is also Hinduism, Moslem and even Buddhism, but the reason why I left Haiti and came to these shores was because of the religious movements that began homogenising elements of both Christianity and West African heritage. This fascinated me the most. They concentrated on spirit possessions, drumming, riveting dancing, all so very similar to Haiti. Obeah it was called, thought to be the birth of Africa. Now Revivalism seems to be growing. I am not too sure what that is; a combination of Christianity and meditation, aided by cannabis consumption and the demand for social reform, all delivered using great fervour.'

'Yes. I have never heard Rastafarianism described so well,' I replied, impressed.

'Good, I do understand then. It seems to be an important cultural movement, although only represented by a small portion of the population and advocated by the poorer communities.'

The squall calmed and she appeared in front of me. 'And here *you* are, lost in between Barbados and the spirit world.

'The majority of Bajans are Christians, Anglicans to be precise, their inheritance from British colonisers. Lately, pious multiplicities have been flourishing in Barbados, there are now Pentecostal churches as well as Roman Catholics, Jews, Hindus, Moslems and even Bahá'í. The list of religions among these small islands is immense. Some help humanity. Some make it worse. Either way, there are always extended consequences. What is illogical is that most human beings know this and yet continue to put their faith in systems created to control. Humans need to believe in the power of self, it is their most valuable contrivance but you all deny yourselves that, you miss that important factor. You are a race capable of extraordinary feats, of knowing the difference between right and wrong but you persist in hurting each other and destroying your environment, all for the short term, often personal gains. I know, I have tested your species numerous times and still you believe falsely, choose badly. There is so much more knowledge, more history you ignore and suppress, more technology you do not share with each other, more medicine you hold back from those needing it the most.' She paused. 'When will you all understand that with unification and cooperation, love and respect for everything around you, as a species, you can all truly evolve into greatness? I have watched you hunt whales to near extinction and not even for the meat. Men would kill a giant of the sea just to drain the spermaceti organ through the whale's blowhole for no more than the waxy liquid used to illuminate your city street lamps and homes. The bodies are discarded and left to rot. During the hunt, vessels would manoeuvre over a grisly sea of blood, as entire families of incorruptible innocence were wiped out. At its peak, this murderous avarice amassed thirty million pounds of sperm oil annually. The true cost of this human benefit only served to push humankind into further darkness, their hearts too selfish to realise it.

'Evolved society has recognised the misdeeds of such grotesque behaviour and many of your species have come together to right this wrong. It is only because you are contemporaneous with this modernity that I am giving the human race another chance.'

I was horrified by what she shared. Delighting in my horror, she smirked and glided back away from me before continuing.

'Documented history is filled with many lies, undoubtedly by the victors, the ones with the power to manipulate and document their side of events. Disappointingly, almost all of human history consists of lies, and the deceit continues to this day. Frankly, unity amongst all species may never come to pass, yet some continue to strive for it. You look puzzled,' she said. 'Do you not agree?'

'My lack of uncertainty is over you. I was led to believe you would be hateful and malicious, but so far, that is not what I am experiencing.'

'Let me guess. Bones?' she asked.

All I could do was nod my head, it seemed pointless to be untruthful at this moment. This Apu glided in so close to me I could feel my skin prickle, her icy breath in my ear as she purred a malicious secret designed to provoke. She turned and moved away. 'Yes, Bones would try and besmirch my name. Never mind.'

'You appear very noble. Knowing all that you know, how could you have tortured Gang Gang Sarah as you did?' I quietly asked, somewhat disappointed.

'I was harsh with her, was I not, but what she did could not go unpunished.' A tone of sadness infiltrated her words. 'You must travel to Haiti. Once there, I will show you the way, if you still wish.'

'Why Haiti?'

'You must retrieve the Staff of Hope, then come to my tomb.' She spoke more tenderly now. 'Once there, do nothing.'

'What is the staff for? Can it open your tomb?'

'I am not actually trapped. My only desire is that you restore my hope in humanity, show me that you are not all lost. After arriving with the staff I will tell you where Ayiti's grave is hidden and only then will I reveal your true purpose. Follow your intuition and *do not* trust easily. Nothing is as it seems.'

My head was spinning, my mind filled with dubiety. She was right, I had trusted Bones all too quickly.

'You *must* go to Haiti,' she said firmly once more. 'Haiti has no official religion, and the constitution, like many allows for religious freedom. If only freedom was something truly tangible. Despite the hollowness of this powerful word and concept, it still comes at a grave price. It was not so long ago that Haiti, one country out of many, paid that price the dearest. The country fought fiercely for their independence and was severely punished by both France and the rest of the world, simply for wanting this said freedom. Many may think this victory was not a success, or so it may seem, but imagine how elated they must have felt, having defeated their oppressors.'

'I don't understand. What battle was Haiti involved in?'

'I think most people would ask that same question,' she solemnly replied. 'Long before Christopher Columbus rediscovered Haiti in 1492, the island had been known by several Taino names, one being Ayiti.' Her eyes flashed at me. 'No, Ayiti's body is not in Haiti but the tools you need are. Before the name Haiti was given in 1804, under the 1697 Treaty of Ryswick, Spain officially ceded the western three-eighths of Hispaniola to France, who renamed the colony Saint-Domingue. This profitable holding produced sugar, coffee, indigo, and cotton, becoming France's wealthiest overseas colony. It was achieved completely through the brutal servitude of innocent human beings perceived to be of an inferior species. By 1803 and after several revolutions, these formidable slaves were finally free, their freedom not given but instead triumphantly won through battles with their rapacious captors. Painfully, their victory was short-lived. Not long after, France formed a blockade to penalise the victors and Saint Dominigue was no longer allowed to trade with the rest of the world. After all, why should these second class human beings or "negroes" be allowed freedom?

'Poverty grew severely, due to the unjust trade restrictions followed by many years of bullying. Propaganda of the highest order was created by the western powers and grew swiftly to discredit these brave souls and their beliefs. Vodou was proclaimed evil, it was declared as having been the main tool used to orchestrate the uprisings. Even today descendants of the insurrection are still demonised by the same propaganda. The beleaguerment was finally lifted only after Haiti agreed to pay remunerations back to France for the loss of their plantations and slave labour. France, a powerful nation, extorted compensation for many years for its once slave-owning squatters, bringing the small broken country and economy to its knees.

'Even though religious freedom is allowed there today, Vodou is looked upon as fictional and its worshipers classed as dark and unclean. It is a religion in which the gods or iwa are derived from West African beliefs and is much older than many other practiced religions. What I find most amusing is that all religion falls into this fictional category as there is not a single shred of academic evidence to prove otherwise, just speculations and "Chinese whispers" built up, embellished, and manipulated over the years. Despite the practice of various *good* religions and slavery being abolished here in this country, you will still find many child slaves to this day.'

I could feel the pain in her voice, see it in her eyes as she revealed these disturbing facts.

Freedom

The power or right to act, speak, or think as one desires.

Kai then added with a mixture of disgust and disappointment evident in his voice, 'Do you know that now in 2016, the International Labour Organisation estimates that forced labor generates an estimated one hundred and fifty billion US dollars in illegal profits each year? Modern-day slavery, enumerated by all its segments, is one of the world's most profitable infractions of the law. The pitiful fact is, that society there in Haiti and in the western world are aware of this problem and yet we tolerate and turn a blind eye towards it, just as humanity has always done in response to many atrocities, using selfish justification as their shield against guilt. In Haiti, despite the efforts of the Restavec Freedom Foundation there are an estimated three hundred thousand child slaves, just in that small country alone. They are labelled as Restavecs, forsaken and without parental care, forced to grow up way ahead of their years and endure the most harrowing circumstances.' Tears running down Kai's face, he faltered. He continued, reverting back to his story.

'The Apu again told me that I would find the tools I needed to retrieve the Staff of Hope right there in Haiti, although the exact location of the staff was unknown.

'You must get the skeletal mask Bones is wearing, be sure to take it with you,' she instructed. 'When you arrive in Haiti you must find a peculiar stone pestle, it is carved with both avian and human images, its main depiction, a bird during an anthropomorphic transformational process. It resides in the Taíno Museum at Route de Labadie, Bande du Nord, Cap-Haïtien. The museum is protected by ancient Taíno spirits. It is imperative that you respect the museum, its artefacts, and the spirits that reside there. The pestle is unique and abnormally powerful, it has been used ceremoniously by the Taíno people for thousands of years. When the relic is in your possession you must trek on this divided isle towards the northern coastline. Caution is required, as the journey within this tortured country will be filled with perils and incomprehensible dangers. Before arriving at the coastline you will encounter a bridge protected by guards that are visible but disguised. You must figure out how to cross on your own. If you survive, the village of Cap-Haïtien awaits on the other side. Search for a small bay known as Caracol. Once there, use the pestle to crush the skeletal mask into a fine powder. Fishermen talk of the struggle to catch fish large enough to create a meal for their families in that destitute bay. Some believe this is because of over-fishing but many are convinced there are sinister forces at work in those waters. You must travel to this remote village and pour the powdered skull into the water. This will release its spirit. Only the gratitude of a soul that was freed from servitude can grant you what you seek.'

Silence followed. Her back towards me, she was truly beautiful.

'Whose soul is trapped within the skull Bones is wearing?' I asked, trying to remain focused.

She responded with a shrug.

'Head hunting has always been misunderstood, and rightly so. Ritualistic decapitations are profoundly immoral and wicked. The practice is done in part to mortify those they wish to suffer, even after death, but mainly because the practitioner feeds on their souls. The victim's essence is trapped in their own skull and sucked by its captor over time as it's worn, but not all is ever drained. Some of it is left behind to ensure the final entrapment, securing the services of the victim as a slave in the afterlife. This is how Bones feeds. No entity should be so evil as to go so far beyond redemption as Bones has.'

'After I free the soul, then what?' I asked.

Without turning around she replied, 'Wait and you may see, seek and you shall find. Remember these words.'

She turned slowly, looking up as though expecting something from the unseeable sky. Instantaneously two items fell from the heavens through the fog; a cane machete with a menacingly sharpened hook on one of its tips; the other item, a small leather pouch in the shape of a— She halted my thought.

'Retrieve them,' her seductive voice demanded of me.

Hesitantly I stooped and picked up the devilish blade, then awkwardly the grim skin bag by its dark flowing ponytail still attached to the dried, shrivelled and unbelievably creepy face, the eyes, nose, and mouth stitch-sealed.

'The pouch is filled with Devil's Breath, an acutely potent toxin which, inhaled or consumed, will turn any person into a zombie. They will do whatever you desire them to. Use it well, without malice or harm towards anyone. The machete is unlike any other blade, it will only destroy demons and will never bring harm to innocence.' She took the machete from me as she said this. Without notice, she swung the angry blade to strike me. I quickly lifted my arm overhead, shielding myself and cowering back, my eyes squeezed shut. The ringing noises of many pieces of metal clinking on the stony floor followed; the blade had shattered into numerous pieces. Opening my eyes to the realisation that I was unharmed, the situation left me astounded. She threw the hilt to me with whatever was left of the blade still attached. I fumbled but caught it. As this god-like apparition in the form of a woman stood there smiling, the blade regenerated in my hand.

'It will never harm purity, but remember, anything pure can always become tarnished.'

As the Apu showed me how overwhelming true understanding could be—is, I remained in an unresponsive stupor. I had expected her mannerisms to portray heartlessness and repel me but her sagacity and beauty, simultaneously compelling, drew me in. The overwhelming presence of this supreme being had my carnality heightened, or was it adrenaline? I required little or no seduction and I felt anything but pure, I wanted to be hers. 'Who are you really?' I had to ask her.

'I am everything and nothing, the wind, the air, the dirt and the seas. Yes, I was once Annie Palmer, and the Aztecs called me Pachacuti. I have always been here and had many different names, even longer than time could remember. My story is a story of ancient and misunderstood origins. I am the circumpunct, the dark swirling heart at the centre of your galaxy. In the beginning, there was light and I gave you all life. This is who I am.

'You are all designed and connected by the same space dust which came from the deepest pits of my innermost self. All of humanity is special, but only some of you truly connect to your inner strength and achieve what you were destined for. In your littered ocean you try to call life, you mortal billions reside alone because you have never truly learnt to establish a genuine connection with your surroundings and each other. Instead, you covet materialism, you fight for it tenaciously as though it will be your salvation when you return to my bosom once more.'

She was right, I have always felt alone. I was alienated and equally, I purposely detached myself. The majority of individuals I encountered in my daily life seemed pretentious, selfish, greedy or just plain loathsome, making it almost compulsory to remain unfastened to society. Her words reverberated, reminding me of this over and over. I really do feel singular on this unilluminated and polluted planet. I knew even before she spoke that I felt differently about most things and I have always felt chastised for it. I was once diagnosed by a friend as having a pathological lack of empathy because I laughed at a speech made by a pontiff encouraging individuals to be more generous human beings. What I found amusing was that the goading came from a man who normally stands and waves from his supreme balcony behind high walls, surrounded by centuries of stolen opulence and history, which they have continually refused to share with the rest of the world. I am totally confused. Is that not hypocrisy? The more I listened to her voice, the more I lost hope for mankind, except for Marita, whom I was now quickly failing to recall I had proposed to, less than twenty-four hours ago.

'There I was, thinking I was not as loathsome as everyone else,' Kai murmured.

'Without defiance or hesitation, you must follow your heart and do what you feel is right. Find the staff, return and you will be able to safely rescue Marita. Only then can we both acquire what our saddened hearts truly desire.'

Uncertainty occurred as her fog abruptly drew me closer. Her skin delicate and electric, it brushed against mine as I capitulated to her unscrupulous manipulation, her living fog resonating with her threat.

'Make no mistake, this comes with a warning. If you make me a promise, do not take it back. If you do not honour your word and you prove yourself untrustworthy, you will no longer receive my love. Bones and his witch have put thoughts in your head, dangerously giving the impression that his lies are what actually matter. The truth is, the mask he wore during the ceremony that brought you to me, is the missing piece of your father. He ripped it from your father's body with his bare hands.

Regretfully, you must return now.'

Before I had the opportunity to respond, she pushed me backwards with incredible force. I awoke, naked and cold, lying on the rocky ground in my bodily fluids, still in that familiar cave. Bones and Sarah were sitting by the dying fire. I perched up, one palm on the ground, the other holding my face, the pain in my head unbearable. Slowly I stood, trying to compose myself, picking up the cane machete and grim pouch of Devil's Breath clenched tight, one item in each hand. I looked for my Baccoo on the snaggy ground, the cork of the bottle now lying next to it. The last statement given by the seraphic woman I had just encountered in the spirit world, rang in my ears.

'Sarah said you were too weak,' Bones taunted. 'I must admit, I refused to heed her forewarning. You think Annie to be a butterfly chrysalis, naked and apparently in peril, but she is not.' His voice was now vile and resentful.

'You are right, she seems anything but defenceless,' I replied.

'You should know that instead of a durable disguise such as the silken cocoon moth pupas are enclosed in, butterfly chrysalises survive by appearing like nothing of significance. Some pupae go even further, jolting to ward off unsuspecting interference. Then there are the ones like Annie, abnormally contriving the oddest humming but instead of this being used to dissuade her aggressors, she lures them with the resonating sound within, leaving her prey in a state of complete and utter bewitchment. *You* are her prey.'

'No. You are,' I replied guilefully.

Sarah, showing her teeth, sneered at me viciously.

'You are with her. We know. You speak in your sleep. We will find Ayiti's body ourselves,' she snarled.

As she spoke, three muscular bodies leapt from the same gateway that Bones had appeared from earlier, men from the same tribe on the beach that had ravished the young woman on the sacrificial pole. They all sprang upon me so fast, their shadowy stone knives still glistening with the dim light of the moribund fire. If their tribal bodies and face paint was meant for intimidation, I confess it worked. I was surrounded, with no time to raise the weapon I was clutching. They slashed and stabbed at my body profusely. My blood gushed and poured, it was a bloodbath. No longer gripping their obsidian bush knives, they retreated from their onslaught only when they thought my body could take no more. Even to this day, I cannot remember any pain, just the disgust and realisation of betrayal. It felt as though time had stopped, my body now like a knife rack. As my muscles relaxed I slowly collapsed onto my knees, a state I now know to be called primary flaccidity. My malefic eyes stared at Bones and Gang Gang Sarah as my face and body continued down towards the cold, rough floor. My eyelids without tension remained open, the green ring around my hazel brown eyes glowed brighter as my pupils dilated. The flexibility of my helpless joints caused my jaw to swing down with the misleading similarity of a meteorite steadily falling towards earth. No tension in my face caused my cheek to collapse into my mouth, leaving me looking downright cadaverous. Suspended in space, looking down at myself, the effects of looking into a mirror was undeniable; a fractured mirror, maybe, as it did not reveal the likeness of the being hovering above the corpse. I knew I was dead. Or so I thought.

My reflection fell back into the cold body, my eyes dry and fluttering watching my Baccoo free and helpful, yanking the last knife from my soma, carrying more than his body weight like an ant.

An unbearably heavy burden on my body then followed, crushing me. My mouth immediately filled with seawater. Gargling and choking, more scepticism followed. I was still in the cave but it was now filled with water. In my confusion and uncertainty I could see Bones and Sarah on the other side of the cave, talking. They were not affected by what was happening, nor did they seem to be in the water. It was like two parallel worlds touching.

As a child, I encountered something similar to this. I remember standing in front of a curtain of rain. The side I stood on was dry and unaffected but I could stretch my arm through to the contrasting side as though a magic curtain controlled the heavenly gifts. There I stood, mesmerised for some time, my hand reaching into the wetness. If not for my other senses I would have believed it to be an illusion. It seemed bizarre that this was what I recalled while suffocating in the strangeness within that cheerless cave. Although still paralysed and unable to breathe, I began floating about in this oddity pretending to be water, now a peculiar, glowing, enigmatic blue. A creature began walking towards me through this substance and with a consistent pace; a horseshoe crab. I hated those prehistoric-looking beasts, they resembled vicious cockroaches and looked nothing like crabs. I knew they were harmless but they disgusted me nonetheless. I gaped at it in astonishment. This must be death, I thought, but before I could truly believe what I was trying to convince myself, the creature entered my mouth. Powerless to resist, it forced its way into my body without rejection, my throat and stomach sore from the coarse exoskeleton of the primordial organism moving about inside me as I lost consciousness.

I awoke lying in the same pool of my bodily fluids for the second time that night, only this time it was strangely different. My wounds were completely healed. I felt no pain or discomfort. I rushed to my feet. My machete and pouch were both on the ground in the mess next to my Baccoo, now back in the bottle. I felt utterly rejuvenated and gently crouched down to pick up the items. Bones and Sarah still sat on the stumps on the other side of the dark cave as they had been previously. I walked up to them soundlessly; the element of surprise was mine.

As they realised I was upon them, Bones leapt up frantically. His face still covered by his mask, his eyes glared at me with that memorable vindictive look which I returned right before my blade sang as it sheered through his neck, taking his head completely off. There was no blood, just dried-up and bitter corruption. His head fell to the ground and rolled about before coming to a stop like a dried coconut. Seconds later, his decapitated body was engulfed in small multi-coloured flames. Both Sarah and I stood watching; before we knew it, all that remained was the disintegrating bone ash. The head was altogether a different story; it remained undamaged, wearing the skeletal mask, the eyes still open with the same evil gaze. I dropped the machete and pouch, bending down to retrieve the mask.

'It belonged to your father,' Sarah said.

I, of course, already knew this but did not react. I pulled my father's partial skeleton off the head of the deceiver, forthwith the head ignited in the palm of my hand. There was no pain or retribution from the flames. I watched with great satisfaction as the head smouldered and as the flame died, all the bone ash from his skull, including the remnants of his body, began to melt away, crumbling into a charred dust. Then it blew away without ceremony on the soft constant sea breeze, floating through the cave.

'All go to the same place. All came from the dust and all return to the dust, Ecclesiastes 3:20,' Sarah murmured, as I shook the last of the dirty remains from my hand.

With my father's remains in my other hand, I calmly picked up the deadly machete from the floor and without any doubt nor hesitation I turned the sharp pernicious tool on Sarah. She did not even protest, nor do I think she was going to put up a fight. Instead of striking, I lowered the blade.

'Bones and Ayiti were the ones who gave Tom the means to steal your powers. They also helped him to acquire your sister. You should go back to Tobago and find her.' Although I felt in no way remorseful and certainly she did not deserve my mercy, I could not destroy her; she had been through enough already and her innocent sister continued to suffer. It was over, or so I hoped. In truth, it had only just begun. Now to disencumber Marita.

Walking towards my Baccoo I noticed the still-bloated, lifeless sack. Clenching the Baccoo, machete, obscure pouch and my dad's skull all pressed together against my chest, I relished the drink from the goatskin as I emerged out of that unforgettable cavity, my eyes struggling to adjust to the bright morning sunlight.

The longboat hovered in the water. Papa Bois began walking over to me along the little of the beach that remained unconsumed by the incoming tide. Mama De L'eau was already there; either she did not see us, or she saw us but did not care. Partially perched on the longboat, she had a long golden lock of her sun-kissed hair coiled around her finger; she seemed relaxed, holding a comb in her other hand, waiting. I was terrified of her. Although she was helping us I did not trust her. I relayed my feelings to Papa Bois as he approached.

'You shouldn't,' he said. 'She is known as the devourer of men. She hates us and would wrap herself around us with the crushing power of her coils and enjoy the feast, given half the chance.'

Motionless we stood. I was still very naked, with my body filthy from the ritual and attempted slaughter. I looked like a distant tribal descendant. Both looking towards the vast distance of nothingness, Papa Bois spoke as he dropped my clothes and watch next to me on the sand.

'That cave will do that to you, no one ever ventures out the same. It was something that had to be done, now discombobulated you are no longer. This is who you really are.'

He was right, I was reborn and I knew exactly what I had to do next. I paused for a moment, lost in my own distraction. This was the most mesmerisingly beautiful place I had ever been to. Marita would have loved it here, it was just a bewitching evanescent notion. I felt too unclean to savour it and any thoughts of Marita now, even good ones, certainly made me lugubrious.

I needed a swim to clean myself and proceeded nearer the welcoming curls. My feet sank into the damp sand before being completely soaked. Truly, I knew I was *vamping* but almost knowingly, this little gesture by the cosmos helped ease the way I felt for a fleeting moment.

A delusional smile appeared on my beguiling face, looking down as I wiggled my toes. I think I was trying to distract my emotional state with the slightest form of solace.

On gradually entering the warm waters, nearby I noticed a strangely calmer constituent going out to sea. The already gentle waves along that serene path were practically non-existent so, logically, I invaded in the direction of the deceptive calm. Abruptly, as I penetrated, a violent concealed influence yanked me by my ankles, I was on my *bamsee* and being dragged into what appeared to be an underwater tributary. Within this unexpected confluent was the strangest mixture of day-to-day items; the multifariousness of packaging, that would normally be a part of my intimate purchases, added to my bafflement. The surge was transporting myself and this animated rainbow of discarded objects into the abyss. Abandoned fishing nets and buoys, plastic everything: cups that would normally be given to transfer my drink into when the pub was closing; grocery bags; yellow taping with the word "caution" stamped on in black; even a double-ended dildo wiggled past like a fluorescent eel.

Gulping and choking, kicking and fighting, quickly I was overpowered; I was no match for this awesome force. Completely unaffected by my presence, the angry propulsion was not nearly finished with me, or the rest of its cargo. It carried us deeper into its belly before I was eventually fed through what felt like a funnel-like bottleneck. Like a newborn emerging into a dissimilar world I made an appearance into a large whirling vortex, my head now above the salty Caribbean Sea. Partnered by other offspring made entirely of trash, we emerged out of the same womb. I gasped greedily for that precious vaporised elixir that no living thing can do without.

My siblings and I were not alone. After regaining my breath I soon discovered we were accompanied by an array of the ocean's monsters. Their sizes and variations contrastingly immense, their vivacity more dazzling than the lifelike waterlogged imbalances they were now feasting on. I, and my brothers and sisters, were a banquet for these ocean-dwelling fabulous creatures.

The vortex initially felt as though its impetus was not great, but as I gradually went round, and round, I quickly realised it was unspectacularly insistent, something *I* was not any longer. It was bright no more, the sky was now dark with light on the far horizon in every direction; I could only just see. Land was completely gone, there was now merely sea.

As the binge escalated, their mood becoming more ferocious, the existing whirlpool intensified into a more violent Charybdis. The heavens directly above equally as hectic, a whirlwind of buff-coloured smoke mirroring the liquid swirl I was trapped in but spinning in the opposite direction. It made me alarmingly giddy and as I closed my eyes and began passing out a hand grabbed hold of me, swiftly followed by a familiar voice.

'*Ah got yuh.*'

Night was now upon us in Plymouth, we had been gone almost all of the second half of the day. I must have unconsciously driven us back while engrossed in the story. Parked in the lot at the residential home where Kai was residing, we both calmly sat with the heated seats comfortably on. His final statement sounded distracted, then he stopped talking completely, his attention now utterly preoccupied by the dense fog we were engulfed in. I, on the other hand, more concerned by only one thing. Kai gingerly opened the passenger door and had already been cautiously edging his way out into this sudden murky unknown, but I stayed motionless with a severe frown and a hard gaze in his direction. Stubborn curiosity had its clutches on me and I just had to ask—

Krick krack

Krick krack monkey break'e back fuh ah piece ah pomerac.

Don't know why, but this is how most folk-stories in Trinidad ended when I was a kid.

Jwe ak pè
Thirteen minutes later the fog was gone.

A woman lightly pushed through the chained curtain of the kitchen doorway on the ground floor. The sensor lights above the entrance immediately illuminated the open space leading to the car park. Taller than average, she wore nude heels and a beige pencil dress which hugged her slender physique. Her calm gait halted before she was completely free, the cold chains brushing against the muscle definition of her exposed calves as she froze.

'Something's wrong,' she whispered.

She could see her Tesla parked with the driver's and front passenger door open. No one was observable. Her flowing white hair was disturbed by the phone pressed to one ear; no dial tone. Suddenly she moved quickly, with a confident stride towards her vehicle, the click-clack sounds coming to a halt as she got nearer. The backseats were empty, as her piercing green eyes had discovered. Slowly, she awkwardly gyrated, peering into the night. Standing there entirely alone, the sensor lights went out.

Appeal

Although my need of you is now great, my rage is still more.

If only you would realise that enjoying the gift of sunshine together is greater, devouring all within the openness of daylight is not right furthermore.

Hastening my demise will only harm creation.

Tenderness for all of you I still have even now as before, myself a malediction I have given for sure.

Although you pain me I still protect with nature your nations, until the day you are all no more.

D.

We are *all* responsible for hurting all that exists around us, all the time.

This plea for change supports those already fighting to make a difference.

About the Author

Don Fabien, a Trinidadian Scribbler stumbling through life like everyone else. *Cyah spell tuh save e' life—buh could tell ah great tale.*

Don grew up in Fyzabad, a small town in the Saint Patrick County of Trinidad and Tobago. He lived for many years in Manhattan, New York before emigrating to the United Kingdom where he gained a BA (Hons) Business Administration with Plymouth University.